THE MERRY MULDOONS
and the
BRIGHTEYES AFFAIR

A Richard Jackson Book

THE Merry Muldoons

AND·THE

Brighteyes

➤ Affair ◄

Brooks McNamara

ORCHARD BOOKS
New York

Orchard Books
95 Madison Avenue
New York, NY 10016

Manufactured in the United States of America
Book design by Mina Greenstein
The text of this book is set in 12 pt. Caslon 540.

2   4   6   8   10   9   7   5   3   1

Library of Congress Cataloging-in-Publication Data
McNamara, Brooks.
The Merry Muldoons and the Brighteyes affair / by Brooks
McNamara.   p.   cm.
Summary: Two children and their father must hastily
abandon their vaudeville act in the Bowery when a dangerous
thug chases them across the New York countryside to recover
a cache of diamonds.
ISBN 0-531-05454-3.   ISBN 0-531-08604-6 (lib. bdg.)
[1. Criminals—Fiction.   2. Humorous stories.]   I. Title.
PZ7.M47879285Me   1992
[Fic]—dc20   91-46923

For JANE and WHITNEY

• 1 •

ONCE we were all safely back in New York City, my sister, Vera, said I ought to write a book about how we were chased across the state by a lunatic and almost killed half a dozen times. I remember the moment all too clearly. I was sitting at our kitchen table, reading and minding my own business, when Vera erupted through the door of our flat like Mount Vesuvius. She was waving a newspaper.

"I was right all along, Sam," Vera said.

"I never doubted it for a minute," I replied. "Now I'd like to finish this book."

"Of course you would," she continued. "So listen to me."

"Good-bye," I answered.

"It says right here, Sam," she responded, thumping the newspaper down on the table, "that a boy your age just made ten thousand dollars writing an adventure novel."

"Delightful," I replied. "Ask him if he'd share it with us. We need the money badly."

"Pay attention," said Vera. "You miss the point, as usual. You are going to write up the Brighteyes Affair."

"I thought *you* were writing up the Brighteyes Affair."

Vera looked uncomfortable. "I tried," she said. "It didn't work out. I am an actress, not an author. Now it's up to you." Her eyes narrowed a little. "Of course, I will help you. I believe that if we set down our story with the proper attention to high adventure and romance, the serial rights alone will bring in a fortune. Then you and Pa and I will be on easy street, and you can leave show business, if you want to."

As always, Vera had found my vulnerable point. To tell you the truth, I think our story has less to do with high adventure and romance and more to do with the fact that The Merry Muldoons (Pa and Vera and me) have an unusual talent for attracting disaster. But I have to admit I'd do almost anything to get out of show business. I am not cut out for the life. Of course, Pa will never hear of it.

Let me explain. The Merry Muldoons have been more or less employed at various joints on the Bowery in New York City ever since Vera and I were babies. Last spring—the spring of 1893—we were performing at Sweeney's Dime Museum near Canal Street (*Everything Clean, Moral, & Refined. Bring the Whole Family.*). On the ground floor is a penny arcade filled with old slot machines and mechanical pianos. Above the arcade is the *Giant Museum & Menagerie*, featuring a dozen wax figures, a stuffed parrot, and a troupe of smelly and bad-tempered chimpanzees.

On the third floor are the freaks, who sit all day long on platforms around the walls, trying to look as cheerful as they can while they wait for Old Man Sweeney to lecture about them to the customers. After a few moments in the company of The Fat Boy and The Living Skeleton, the audience is herded next door for the *Lavish Full-Stage Extravaganza Offered on the Hour from Ten to Ten Daily.* That's where The Merry Muldoons come in. We *are* the *Lavish Full-Stage Extravaganza*—fifteen minutes of the worst hokum anybody ever foisted on an unsuspecting public. I do a clog dance, Vera sings, and Pa tells moth-eaten jokes in Irish dialect. I do not care to repeat any of them.

Audiences seem to find our act more or less invisible, but it is part of their dime's worth, and mostly they sit through it. Sometimes they even manage a feeble bit of applause at the end. The truth of it is, of course, that The Merry Muldoons have absolutely no talent, individually or collectively, and like any reasonable person I find the whole experience humiliating. But Pa and Vera think we are wonderful, which is probably just as well since the act at least provides us with a paycheck of sorts, together with our sumptuous quarters in the dime museum's attic.

Still, as Pa says, we should be grateful for small favors. Ever since Ma died five years ago, when I was six and Vera was eight, things have been pretty rocky for The Merry Muldoons. Miss Slattery claims that Ma was "the only stabilizing influence" on the three of us and that after her death we "lost our thin veneer of civilization" and began to "sail under the black flag of anarchy." Miss Slattery is the principal of P.S. 2, where Vera and I used to go to school. We don't go anymore. Actually, we didn't go much before, which I always gathered was all right with P.S. 2.

Part of the problem was that I had already learned everything they taught in the first term. There was nothing to it; I just read all the books in the school and I understood them. As I used to tell Miss Slattery, I take no more responsibility for my mental quirk than The Fat Boy and The Living Skeleton do for their uniqueness. But it did lead to a certain amount of frustration after the first few months at P.S. 2, and a good deal of time to kill.

Not that I thought up all those incidents that Miss

Slattery blamed on Vera and me—the flooding of the fourth floor, the bomb, and so on. No, I am stronger on logic than imagination. Imagination is Vera's area. Miss Slattery claims that Vera "does not live in the real world" and that she will "fetch up in state's prison one day." If I am fair, I suppose Miss Slattery may have had a point about Vera not living in the real world. However, I mention it only because, as you will see, this aspect of Vera's personality looms very large in the Brighteyes Affair.

THE STORY BEGINS after our fifth or sixth show on a Saturday, when I was on the second floor, feeding the livestock. I remember leaning out the front window to catch a breath of something that wasn't *eau de chimpanzee*, and seeing a man walking down the Bowery in the direction of the museum. Even by local standards, he was a peculiar sight. He was pale and gaunt, with a mop of frizzy carrot-colored hair protruding from under a caved-in top hat, and a shabby suit of clothes two or three sizes too big for him. His eyeglasses were thick slabs of greenish glass that caught the light and reflected it in circles around his beady little eyes. All in all, he looked like a slightly demented circus clown.

The man slowed down just below me in front of Sweeney's and peered at the posters. He seemed to be searching for something. At the same moment, there was a buzz of music from one of the ancient mechanical pianos inside, and Old Man Sweeney stepped out on the sidewalk and began his pitch to the crowd.

"Right this way, ladies and gentlemen," Sweeney bellowed to the two or three people on the sidewalk. "See the amazing educational exhibits—see Madame Ramona and Her Serpents, see General Rhinebeck the Military Midget, and see those Masters of Melody and Mirth, The Merry Muldoons."

The odd-looking man stopped dead in his tracks. "The Merry Muldoons work here, do they?" he said in a high-pitched Irish brogue. It was not precisely a question. "This Muldoon, is he a sort of half-witted fellow, with two brats in tow?"

"Sounds like them, all right," said Sweeney. "Though I wouldn't call what they do *work* exactly. You can find them upstairs in the the-ayter—third floor." He paused and considered the man uneasily. "Friends of yours, are they?"

"You might say that."

"Then you wouldn't mind paying ten cents to see them."

"Ah, but I would," said the man as he passed inside. "I definitely would."

Sweeney, who was a veteran of thirty years on the Bowery, obviously knew when to let well enough alone. He went back to his pitch. "Step right up, ladies and gentlemen. See Homer Neumiller the Human Fire Alarm."

It struck me that Pa might like some advance notice about his visitor, and I sprinted up the stairs to the third floor. Pa and Vera were in what passed for our dressing room. Both of them were snoring away on the floor. "Pa," I said, "there is a very strange man looking for you."

"Stow it," Pa muttered. "I'm asleep."

Just then the man appeared in the open doorway. I gave Pa a nudge with my foot, and he rolled over and opened his eyes. Then he sat bolt upright, and for a moment I thought he was having some sort of fit. His mouth opened two or three times, but no sound came out of it except for a dry croaking.

"Sure, it's Johnnie Muldoon," said the man with a kind of lunatic cheerfulness. As he spoke, he craned his neck forward toward Pa, apparently trying to bring him into focus through his massive spectacles. "Ain't you pleased to see an old pal, then, Johnnie?" The man advanced into the dressing room just as Vera awoke with a start. She gave a little shriek when she saw him.

The man turned toward Vera and me and surveyed us with much head bobbing and neck craning, creating an effect rather like one of Madame

Ramona's serpents being charmed out of a basket. "And these is the little ones, ain't they?" he said to nobody in particular.

Pa looked downright agitated by this point. "This here," he said, "is Mr. Jimmy Dunphy. We used to know each other in the—er—old days."

"And golden days they was, Johnnie. Golden days, indeed." With that, he broke into a kind of Irish jig, flapping about the dressing room in a way that was terrifying to behold.

Pa was looking positively green as the man danced over in my direction. "You can call me Brighteyes," he said, "which is what all my friends call me." Then he grabbed me by the arm. "I think we will be seeing a good deal of each other since your pa and I has been reunited once again. Now, if you children will just excuse us for a moment or two, we will be wanting to talk over old times. You can understand how it is when two pals ain't seen one another for, lo, these many years." He steered us, none too gently, out the door and shut it behind us.

"A little batty in the knob," said Vera as we dropped to our knees next to the keyhole. But Pa and Brighteyes were out of sight and talking too low for us to hear much of anything. After a while, we lost interest and wandered off to watch Homer Neumiller, whose act was just starting next door. A few minutes later, Brighteyes came careening into the freak show. He made his way over to Vera and me and stood behind us, twitching and shuffling.

"Mighty creepy, them freaks," he said.

"Well, I don't think so," I began.

"Look here, mister," Vera said. "They're our friends. Lay off."

But Brighteyes didn't hear us. He was already flapping away toward the stairs, snapping his fingers in time to some jaunty tune that only he could hear.

•2•

A T FIRST I didn't see anything especially remarkable about Pa's encounter with Brighteyes. Before he met Ma, I knew, his choice of friends had led to considerable trouble. The details were a bit hazy, but every now and then someone from those days reappeared in Pa's life, usually departing rapidly with most of our bankroll.

This looked like one of those times. As the day wore on, Pa grew more tense and jumpy by the minute. During our next show, he performed like a sleepwalker. Afterward he sat in the dressing room, saying absolutely nothing, contemplating a spot on the wallpaper.

"Pa," I began, "about that man Brighteyes. You didn't loan him any—"

Pa's response was somewhat tangled. "Stay away from that fella," he said. "He ain't as crazy as he seems to be. That is, he ain't, but he is, but then again he ain't, if you follow my meaning."

"We don't," said Vera.

"Well, there you go," said Pa. "That's just what I'm saying, ain't it?"

This seemed to conclude the interview. I beckoned Vera out into the hall.

"Did you notice whether Pa still has his pocket watch and ring?" I asked. These were usually the first to go when Pa's old pals showed up.

"Both still there," she replied. "And all of Pa's money is still on the dressing table—about a dollar seventy-five, give or take a few cents. Very puzzling. Who do you think that strange man is?"

"Just one of Pa's deadbeat friends, I suppose."

"I'm not so sure about that," she said warily. "I'm not so sure this time. . . ."

"Leave it alone, Vera," I replied. "We have enough troubles already."

Just then Pa appeared in the doorway. He handed Vera fifty cents for our suppers and went out without saying another word to either of us. When he arrived back for the six o'clock show, he smelled of whiskey, but he seemed more composed. As the evening wore on, Pa's mood improved a good deal, thanks to a bottle concealed in a fire bucket outside the dressing-room door. Our last show, at ten o'clock, for an audience of four, went fairly well, all things considered, and I was beginning to feel a bit cheerier myself. I should have known better.

"Run along upstairs," Pa said to us, with elaborate casualness. "I've got some business to attend to."

Vera didn't respond, merely humming "There's a Land That Is Fairer Than Day" in a manner I recognized as dangerous. As we left the dressing room, Pa was staring at a spot on the wallpaper again. I don't think he even heard us go.

I started upstairs. Suddenly, my head whipped backward as Vera grabbed me by the collar. "Not that way," she whispered. "Follow me." She dragged me down to the street and behind one of the columns that supports the elevated railway that runs along the middle of the Bowery.

"Why are you doing this to me?" I inquired. "I want to soak my feet."

"We're going to follow Pa, of course," Vera replied.

"You may be, but I'm going home. This is none of our business and—"

"Hush!" Vera whispered. "He's coming out of the museum now."

Sure enough, there was Pa, heading north up the Bowery. For some reason, he was wearing his winter overcoat, a shabby black affair that reached to his shoe tops. Pa kept glancing over his shoulder nervously as he fell in with the people milling around in front of the shooting galleries and dance houses.

Vera grabbed me by the collar again and pulled me into the crowd.

"I think this is a terrible mistake," I said. "But I don't suppose I have any choice."

"Absolutely none," Vera replied. "Now be quiet."

We saw Pa turn west on Fourteenth Street into the theater district, where there were even bigger crowds because the shows were just letting out for the night. At the big opera house, the Academy of Music, he turned north again into Irving Place. The crowd thinned considerably there, and we had to drop back a bit and stick to the shadows as he headed toward Gramercy Park.

Gramercy Park is an elegant private square enclosed by a high iron fence and surrounded by some of the fanciest houses in the city. It was not exactly where you would expect to find Pa. But there he was on the sidewalk near the southwest corner, leaning up against the fence. Vera and I hung out in a doorway down the block.

Pa apparently believed that he was in some sort of disguise. The temperature was close to ninety, and the sky was split by ragged streaks of heat lightning. But the collar of his long, heavy overcoat was turned up around his ears, and his plug hat was pulled down so that the brim rested on his eyebrows.

Every few seconds, he would drag his watch out of his vest pocket, click open the cover, and stare at the dial. Then he would peer up and down the street and, seeing nothing, begin a little pacing dance on the sidewalk—half a dozen steps east and then half a dozen steps west again. All in all, Pa could not have stood out more in Gramercy Park if he had been a Zulu warrior in full battle array.

It wasn't long before Brighteyes appeared, skulking out of a nearby doorway. The two of them talked for a minute or two, with Pa occasionally pointing to a house on the south side of the park and Brighteyes frantically jerking his arm down each time Pa raised it. Then they almost disappeared from our view, as the rainstorm that had been waiting to happen let loose, accompanied by a whole symphony of thunder and lightning.

"I want to hear what they're saying," Vera shouted at me over the downpour.

"We can't get that close."

"Of course we can. We can go through the park."

"There's an eight-foot-high fence around it, idiot," I yelled. "And the gates are chained shut."

"We'll go over the fence. Come on. Lots of footholds. Nothing to it."

In a twinkling, as they say, Vera was on top of the fence and starting to climb down the other side. I followed. After eight or ten unsuccessful tries in which I lost the knees of both my knickers and most of the skin on one hand, I dropped down next to her.

I followed Vera as she headed down the center of the park toward Pa and Brighteyes, working her way from bush to bush and tree to tree, spy style. There wasn't much danger of us being seen or heard, because of the storm, and we dashed the last few feet to a hiding place in a bush only about a yard away from them. Just as we got there, Brighteyes moved away from the fence and started across the street toward the house that Pa had been pointing at.

The house was a grand affair, five stories high, with basement windows at sidewalk level and a steep flight of steps leading up to the front door on the main floor. In a moment, Brighteyes was standing next to a basement window. The house was pitch-dark, but there was a streetlamp nearby, and I could see him pull a sack from his overcoat pocket, haul out a jimmy or crowbar of some sort, and approach the window. Then my view was blocked by his body. But it was clear what was going on, and in less than a minute he had raised the sash, unlatched the shutters that covered the window on the inside, and disappeared into the house.

Meanwhile, Pa was repeating his nonchalant routine, uncorking his watch every ten seconds or so and peering wildly up and down the street. If there had been any doubt before, it was obvious now that Brighteyes was using poor Pa as lookout while he burgled someone's house.

As I pondered this, the whole square was rocked

by a tremendous explosion. When I got up the courage to peek out from behind our bush, I could see that the glass in the mansion's basement windows had evaporated and smoke was beginning to billow out into the street.

Before I could grab her, Vera bounded from behind the bush, calling Pa's name. I thought he was going to collapse on the spot, but Vera grabbed him through the bars of the fence and brought his face up to hers. "It's us, Pa. It's Vera and Sam."

Pa seemed not to hear. "My heart's gave out," he babbled. "I'm done for."

"Pa," Vera yelled, "get out of here. Run!"

He lurched back against the bars and stared at her in horror. Then, suddenly, he seemed to come to his senses. "All right. Let's go."

"We can't, Pa. We have to climb the fence. Just go. Meet us at home." Pa hesitated. "Go!" Vera shrieked.

Pa nodded to her, then turned and ran wildly in the direction of Irving Place. As he rounded the corner, Brighteyes appeared in one of the blown-out windows. He stumbled halfway out, almost falling flat, and leaped to the sidewalk. Vera and I just had time to drop back behind our bush before he sprinted across the street to the spot where Pa had been standing. I could see that he still had the sack in his hand.

Brighteyes called out to Pa in a hoarse whisper,

"Johnnie! Johnnie Muldoon! Where the devil are you? I got it."

Just then, there came the sound of a window being slammed open somewhere nearby and a woman's voice screaming, "Fire! Fire!" In a minute, I could hear shouting and doors opening nearby. From a little way off came the sound of a fire bell. People began to flood into the street, heading for the smoke—and Brighteyes. He called out for Pa again. "Muldoon! Take the sack, or you're a dead man." But Pa was long gone.

The whole basement floor of the house was burning now. By the light of the flames, I could see Brighteyes hesitate a second and then heave the sack over the fence and into our bush. It struck me full on the head.

"Urrgh!" There was something heavy inside the sack, and I gasped when it hit me.

Vera clapped her hand over my mouth. "Shhh," she hissed.

Brighteyes paused and peered intently in our direction, obviously wondering what he had heard. After a moment, he seemed satisfied that there was nothing wrong, and I watched him scuttle around the corner of the park, heading north, away from the burning mansion and out of sight.

·3·

WE WATCHED Brighteyes disappear and then scrambled around in the mud to see what he had pitched into our hiding place. It turned out to be a greasy old flour sack. Inside it were the jimmy he had used to pry open the window, a two-dollar pistol, and one of those little tin boxes about the size of your hand that people use to hold stamps and coins. It was locked and it rattled a little when I shook it.

Vera eyed the box with interest. "Open it," she said.

"I can't. There isn't any key. And besides, it doesn't belong to us. Let's leave it and get out of here."

"Wait a minute," Vera said, ignoring me completely. "I want to see if I can force the lock. Hand me the jimmy."

"No," I said. "Brighteyes was obviously expecting to pass this stuff over to Pa. He'll be back for it, and I don't want to be here when he arrives."

"Nonsense," Vera said. "He wouldn't dare come back for hours. Look at all the people out there in the street."

"I am," I said, "and one of them is Brighteyes."

"What?"

"Over by the fire engine." Sure enough, he had doubled back for another look. There he was, twenty feet away from us, apparently watching the firemen like any solid citizen. In fact, his eyes were glued on Vera and me. He took a casual step or two in our direction.

"Why didn't you tell me?" Vera inquired.

"I just did. Now drop the bag, and let's get out of here."

"Right," said Vera. She started to run north across the park, the bag firmly clutched in her hand. I took off after her. This time I made it over the fence before she did.

"What should we do?" I asked.

"I think we may have lost him," Vera replied. "Let's just go home quick."

It was true that Brighteyes was nowhere to be seen, so we ran straight south toward the Bowery. After five or six blocks, we hit Fourteenth Street again and stopped to catch our breath. We were still close to Irving Place, and I could smell the smoke drifting down from the burning house on Gramercy Park.

"Step in here for a moment," Vera said. We were just passing the alley that runs alongside the Academy of Music. She pulled me into the alley and began to dump out the contents of the flour sack on the cover of an ash barrel.

"What in heaven's name are you doing?" I inquired.

It became apparent that what she was doing was attacking the little tin box with the jimmy once again. "I've got to know what's in here," she said as she pried vigorously away at the lock.

I peered around the corner of the alley just in time to see Brighteyes pop out of a doorway a few yards away. Of course he had managed to follow us after all. I recalled Pa's comment that the man was not as crazy as he seemed to be, and it began to make increasing sense. I slunk back into the alley and tapped Vera on the shoulder.

"Sister, dear," I whispered, "I think there is someone here to see you."

She glanced up from her work. "What are you talking about?" I watched her eyes travel to the end of the alley where, in the glow from the streetlamp, a giant shadow had appeared on the wet sidewalk.

"I wonder who it could be?" I asked.

"Just some passerby," Vera replied. But she sounded rather tentative, and I noticed that she was rapidly dumping Brighteyes's gear back in the bag.

"Then why isn't he passing by?"

"Let's head up the alley in the other direction," Vera whispered. "Just in case."

"It's a dead end."

The shadow began to move with considerable speed, and I found myself suddenly enfolded in a bear hug, with Brighteyes on the outside. "What a coincidence," he said. "I've been wanting to have a word with you for ages. About the box. I'll be taking it now, before the accident."

"What accident?"

"The accident that is going to happen to both of you after you give me the box." He pulled a knife out of his pocket and flicked it open in the vicinity of my right ear. "I think we'll begin with the little fellow. First a little nick here"—he demonstrated on my earlobe—"and a little nick there, and then the main event, if you take my meaning." I did.

"All right," Vera hissed as she reached into the bag, "you can have it. It's right here."

"No tricks, now," said Brighteyes.

Vera pulled out Brighteyes's pistol and pointed it at him. "Let him loose," she said, "and drop the knife."

Brighteyes reflected for a moment, tossed the knife on the ground, and backed away a step or two. "Be careful with that thing," he said.

"Now, then," Vera continued. "Just stay where you are while Sam ties you up." She pointed to a hunk of decayed rope hanging from a drainpipe.

"What do you mean, 'while Sam ties you up'?" I said, dabbing at my wounded ear. "If you're so crazy about tying him up, give me the gun and you do it. You got us into this. And besides, I'm bleeding."

"One little scratch," Vera said, "and you go into a decline. I'll handle it. You just amuse yourself, as usual, and I'll take care of everything." At this point, Vera and I were on our way to a full-scale argument and paying no attention to Brighteyes. As he was merely crazy, not an idiot, he reached over, took the gun out of her hand, and grabbed me again.

"Run!" I yelled. "Save yourself!" I didn't mean it.

Vera paid no attention anyway and came charging in our direction, swinging the flour sack around her head like David drawing a bead on Goliath. I saw what she had in mind and lunged forward, coming down hard with my foot on Brighteyes's instep just as Vera connected with the bag containing the jimmy and the box. It struck him square on the forehead, and he staggered back into a stack of trash barrels, sending them crashing down on himself. I struggled free.

From somewhere inside the pile, Brighteyes let out a fairly ghastly moan, followed by a series of grunts and mumbles and swear words. Vera and I did not wait around to listen. We headed sedately out of the alley, smiled politely at the watchman from the Academy of Music, who was just returning with a bucket of beer in his hand, and were off and running down Fourteenth Street again in the direction of the Bowery.

·4·

ERA AND I didn't stop until, gasping for breath, we ran inside Sweeney's and bolted the door behind us.

It was pitch-dark in the arcade, and we inched our way across the floor in the direction of the stairs. About halfway there, I stepped on Old Man Sweeney's cat, which rose straight up in the air like a Fourth of July rocket and came down on the front of my shirt. I backed up into Vera, who collided with one of the mechanical pianos, starting it off on "The Widow Nolan's Goat."

"It's Brighteyes!" Vera yelled.

"It's the stupid cat!" I yelled back. "Get it off me!"

Vera amputated the cat from my chest and heaved it into the darkness just as the piano began to launch into "Love's Old Sweet Song."

We finally made it to the hall outside our flat in

the attic. Neither of us had a key, and the door was firmly locked. I knocked cautiously.

"It's Vera and Sam, Pa. Let us in."

There was a rumbling inside the flat as Pa dismantled some sort of barricade. He opened the door a quarter of an inch and peered at us through the crack. "Get in here," he hissed. "I've been waiting for you for hours." We didn't have to be coaxed. We slipped inside, helped Pa reassemble the barricade in front of the door, and quickly filled him in on our late unpleasantness with Brighteyes.

"Please, Pa, let's get out of here," I said. We may have had a fair lead on Brighteyes, but it was a sure thing he knew we lived in the museum and that he would be along for a visit soon.

"Hold on, Sam," Vera said as she rummaged through a dresser drawer. She sounded preoccupied, which made me nervous. After a bit of a search, she pulled out a ring of old keys.

I knew right away what she had in mind. One of the keys would open the cheap lock on the little tin box. "Don't do it," I said. "I don't want to see whatever it is."

Vera was already dumping the box out of the flour sack onto the kitchen table. When Pa saw it, he began to look distinctly ill. "Don't open it," he said. "Let it alone."

The third key worked, and there was a little pop

as the lid snapped open. I couldn't help myself. I looked inside. The box was almost filled with diamonds, hundreds of them, winking up at me in the light from the lamp that hung over the table.

"Close the lid," Pa said. "I can't bear it."

Vera stirred the diamonds absentmindedly with her forefinger.

"Forget it," I said. "If we keep those diamonds, Brighteyes will kill us."

She picked up a particularly handsome specimen and examined it minutely. "I think he has already tried," she said. "But he's crazy. Who knows what he'll do?"

"I may pass out," said Pa, reaching over to open the window next to the kitchen table. Suddenly, he leaped back as though the window were on fire. "Quick!" he whispered. "Put out the light."

Vera looked at him strangely, but she did what he asked. I went to the window and peered out from behind the curtain. It had begun to rain again, but I could see well enough to recognize Brighteyes standing on the sidewalk, bloody but apparently unbowed. Vera joined me at the window. Perhaps Brighteyes knew that we were watching him, because he looked in our direction and seemed to touch his battered old hat in a grisly greeting. Or maybe he didn't. But there he was on guard duty outside the museum, leaning against a lamppost, his coat collar turned up against the weather, chewing on a soggy cigar.

"We're leaving now," said Vera.

"Good idea," I responded. "But just how do you plan to do it? The door to the alley is nailed shut so that patrons can't duck out when they see how bad Sweeney's dump really is, and Brighteyes is planted in front of the only door to the street."

Vera thought it over. "All right," she said, "we'll go across the roofs."

That sounded fine to me. The museum is at the end of a block-long row of buildings. Each one is attached to its next-door neighbor, so it is possible to get from one roof to another without much trouble. Vera and I had done it dozens of times. The beauty of it was that on every roof there is a little shed that covers the top of that building's stairway. In theory, all Pa and Vera and I had to do was to find one of the sheds that was unlocked, creep down the stairs, and walk out on the street, maybe almost a block away from Sweeney's—and from Brighteyes.

While I was thinking it over, Vera was crashing about in the half-light from the window, throwing our possessions into a valise and an old carpetbag she had found under Pa's bed. In ten minutes or so, she had gathered up everything worth carrying and stowed it in the two bags, with space left over.

"Let's go," she said.

"Not until you promise to leave the diamonds here," I answered. "Let Brighteyes have them."

"That goes double for me," Pa added.

Because the light was so bad, it was hard to tell exactly what Vera's reaction was. She looked at us oddly, I thought, and then burrowed into the carpetbag for a moment and slammed the box down on a dresser.

"All right," she said. "Anything to get out of here." She shooed us from the room into the hall and closed the door firmly behind her. Then she dashed up the stairs that led to the roof, with Pa and me lurching after her, bags in hand. It crossed my mind that Vera had given up a bit easily. But at the moment, I was too frightened to think about it very hard.

Once we were on the roof, I crept over to the Bowery side and had a look into the street. There was no Brighteyes, which was not especially reassuring. I crawled over to Pa and Vera, who were waiting by the stairs, huddled together against the rain, and the three of us took off across the rooftops. After several false starts, we found an unlocked door on the roof of Morrisey the undertaker's place, which seemed in keeping with the whole spirit of the evening. Pa and Vera and I headed downstairs.

As we hit the ground floor, there was an ominous series of clunks and rumbles from the roof that suggested that Brighteyes had probably broken into the museum and picked up our trail again. We took off, running west along Canal Street through the downpour. After five minutes or so, I was struck by an unnerving thought.

"Hold it," I said. "Where are we going?"

Pa and Vera looked blank. The subject had not really come up before.

"Let me put it another way," I continued. "How much money do we have?"

The three of us retreated into a doorway and counted our cash, which as usual was less than we had thought.

"Well," I said, "I suppose this means Aunt Gussie's again." Gussie is Ma's great-aunt in Brooklyn. She is known in the family as The Gorgon, and we have stayed with her at various humiliating moments in the past.

"Oh, no, not that," said Pa.

"I absolutely refuse," Vera replied. "Not after what she said to me last time."

"Well," I said. "Any other ideas?"

Vera seemed to be stumped for once. Pa looked thoughtful. "I suppose we could go to Uncle Mike's," he said, "but we ain't got the money to get that far." Uncle Mike Muldoon is Pa's brother, who has risen to great heights in politics and the saloon business in Poughkeepsie. Uncle Mike would probably not welcome our visit. He had pointed out on several previous occasions that we were a threat to his social standing. But he probably would not throw us out on the street either. Vera, who still seemed somewhat preoccupied, nodded her approval.

"Fine," I said. "Let's get as close as we can to Poughkeepsie and worry about the rest of it later." There was no Brighteyes in evidence, and we struck out in the direction of the elevated railway. We hopped off as the train rolled into Grand Central Station, and ran for the ticket booths.

"Is there a train leaving soon for Poughkeepsie?" I asked the clerk at the only ticket window open at this ungodly hour of the morning.

"Ought to be. It's a railroad station, ain't it?" replied the clerk, who was industriously inspecting his fingernails.

"All right," I answered. "*When* does the next train leave for Poughkeepsie?"

"Five minutes." He returned to his fingernails. "Hudson River line."

I shoved all of our money over the counter in the clerk's direction. "How far will this take us? One way."

He stared at the money for a while and then counted it ten or twelve times. Finally, he put on a green eyeshade and counted it again.

I was in agony as I watched the hands of the station clock move in the direction of train time. "Excuse me," I said, "but how close to Poughkeepsie can we get with this money?"

"Don't know yet," the man said as he rummaged behind the counter. At length, he came up with a ledger that he consulted for several centuries, with much page turning and head scratching.

"Cold Spring," he said at last.

"I beg your pardon?"

"Cold Spring. You can get as far as Cold Spring. It's a little burg up in Putnam County. Ain't much going on there."

"Fine," I said. "We'll take three for Cold Spring."

"Right," said the clerk, who had gone back to his fingernails.

We made the train with seconds to spare. I looked back as we climbed aboard and thought I saw someone who looked like Brighteyes stroll out on the platform. But the light was poor, so I couldn't be sure about it. Anyway, just then the train started up, much to my relief. Instantly, Pa was snoring.

"Lend me your comb," Vera said.

"Where's yours?" I replied.

"I left it back at the flat, along with the rest of my toilet articles."

Everything came into focus now. "I see," I

gasped. "Together with that little tin box in which you kept them."

"Correct," said Vera.

"You switched boxes?"

"Correct again," Vera responded, pulling the box out of the carpetbag. She opened the lid and began to fondle the diamonds. "I didn't think you'd fall for such an obvious trick, but then we were all under pressure. However, thanks to me and these beautiful diamonds, our future is now secure."

"That's a laugh," I said. "Brighteyes will follow us to the ends of the earth to get them back. Thanks to you and those rotten diamonds, we're as good as dead already."

·5·

"PA! WAKE UP," I cried, shaking him. "Vera's got the diamonds."

"Hush, you little snitch," she said. "There are more important matters to discuss." Vera turned to Pa. "You have to explain what's going on."

Pa, whose face had turned an unusual shade of purple, did not seem pleased at my news. He gasped and sputtered for a while, then finally began to recover himself, and this is what he told us as our train headed north along the Hudson River.

"It ain't a pretty story," he began. "I met Brighteyes when I was about your age, just after I landed in New York. It become clear pretty quick that he was some kind of nut case, and I tried to stay clear of him as much as I could. But you know how Brighteyes is—he never lets up—and he dogged me night and day to join him in some scheme he had in mind.

Finally, I said I'd do it, whatever it was, just to be rid of him.

"I didn't think no more about it until he come to my room one night. He looks at me and says, 'Johnnie, my lad, tonight's the night you and me become millionaires and give work the horselaugh for the rest of our lives.'

"I says, 'If it's all the same to you, Brighteyes, I'll just hang around the room tonight and read a good book or two. But you feel free to go on without me.'

"Well, Brighteyes laughs a lot at that. Then he grabs me hard by the arm and shoves me out the door, and I know I don't have no choice but to go with him.

"He runs us up and down back alleys for half an hour or so until he is sure nobody is following us. Then he stops and says to me, 'I can tell you now, Johnnie. We is going to rob Mother Mandelbaum and make the coppers think somebody else done it.'

"I know the old hag he is talking about. 'I'd rather die,' I says.

" 'That's a strong possibility,' he replies, 'unless I have your complete cooperation.' To make his point clear, he pulls out a pistol and holds it to my head.

"It's about then I figure I am a goner, for certain,

because if Brighteyes don't kill me, then it's a sure thing that Mother Mandelbaum will. Mother is the biggest fence in New York—handles more stolen goods than all the rest of them put together—and the toughest. She'd shoot Brighteyes and I down like dogs in case of the slightest misunderstanding, and it seems likely that there is about to be a *serious* misunderstanding.

"Anyways, Brighteyes tells me his plan, and my blood runs cold at the very thought. 'Johnnie,' says he, 'what do you see here in my hand?'

" 'A pistol,' I says, 'and I wish you would put it away.'

" 'No, you dunce,' he says, 'in my other hand.'

"I look, and it is a ordinary man's leather wallet, for keeping your money in. Brighteyes hands it to me, and I open it, and there is a name wrote inside like people do. It says *Michael Aloysius Connelly*.

" 'Well?' says Brighteyes.

" 'Well, what?' I says.

" 'You dodo,' says Brighteyes. 'That there belongs to Baboon Connelly. I pinched it from him a few days ago.'

"Now, I know who Baboon Connelly is. Him and his brother Apeneck is pals of Brighteyes. People says one of them is a half-wit, though it is hard to tell which one they mean. I can imagine that it ain't much trouble to steal something from either of them, but I can't see what Brighteyes has in mind. 'Baboon never has no money,' I says, 'so why would you bother to take his pocketbook?'

" 'Why, you fool,' says he, 'so we can leave it beside Mother Mandelbaum's body after we robs her safe and murders her.'

" 'Oh, I got it now,' I says.

" 'And then,' Brighteyes goes on, 'we clear out for Canada and a ship bound for foreign ports, with a fortune in our pockets, while the coppers is hunting down Baboon for the murder of Mother Mandelbaum.' Then he starts laughing fit to be tied, tears rolling down his cheeks at the beauty of it all.

"Meanwhile, I'm shaking in my shoes because, no matter what he says, I am sure Brighteyes has plans for me even worse than what he has thought up for poor Baboon Connelly. Pretty soon, Brighteyes calms down a bit and tells me what we are going to do. He has stole half a dozen bolts of silk somewhere and stashed them in an alley nearby. He says we is to pretend it is loot we want Mother to buy from us, and when she opens up her safe to get out the money to pay us, he will shoot her. Then we will drop Baboon's pocketbook, pack up everything in the safe, and be on our way.

"To tell you the truth, I don't think Mother Mandelbaum will fall for such a harebrained scheme, and nobody in his right mind would've thought so either. But there we is, five minutes later, knocking on the door of her house. I figure for a while that I'm saved because she don't seem to be at home. Then I see there's a lamp lit inside, and Brighteyes, he sees it too and shoves on the door. It creaks open with a horrible sound, and there in the front room I can see Mother sprawled out across a table.

" 'Let's go,' I says. 'She's already murdered—somebody got in ahead of us.'

"Brighteyes, he sniffs the air a bit and then turns and gives me a disgusted look. 'No, you moron,' he says, 'she's been smoking opium and is out like a light. She won't wake up for hours. But the safe is locked.'

"I look into the corner where the safe is standing and, sure enough, I can see that he is right.

" 'Wait a minute,' he says. 'What have we got here?' He's pointing at the little tin box laying next to Mother's head. 'Do you suppose she was doing some business before she conked out?' He turns the key in the lock and flips open the lid with the barrel of his pistol, and there they is—the diamonds, just like you seen them last night.

" 'Hallelujah!' Brighteyes yells. 'I'm a rich man after all.' I notice that he don't bother to say 'we' this time, which don't improve the state of my nerves very much. But I manage to suggest that we leave now.

" 'Hold on,' says he. 'I ain't nailed the old woman yet.'

" 'Don't do it, Brighteyes,' I says. 'Please don't do it.' I see him stop for a second or two, thinking it over, and then he begins that crazy laugh again.

" 'I'll just leave the pocketbook,' he says, 'and let Mother Mandelbaum take care of Baboon when she wakes up. Sure, he'll wish it was the coppers before she's through with him. That's a good one, ain't it?'

"I don't suppose that Baboon Connelly will think so, but I don't say nothing, being very concerned at the moment that Brighteyes is intending to leave my corpse in Mother Mandelbaum's parlor along with Baboon's wallet. But he just shoves the pistol into his belt, picks up the box, locks it, and drops the key in his vest pocket. Then he deposits the evidence on the table and skips out the front door, as merry as you please, with a firm hand on my coat collar.

"After a few minutes, it dawns on me that we has left the part of town I am familiar with and is in the neighborhood of Gramercy Park. Now Brighteyes stops in front of the same house you seen last night.

" 'What are we doing here?' I says.

" 'Why, Johnnie,' Brighteyes answers, 'we is going inside like the two society gentlemen we now is.'

"And with that, he hauls out a key and unlocks the ground-floor door and motions me inside. Well, I thinks, at least I'll die rich, which will be a new experience on several counts. So I go in, and Brighteyes, he locks the door after us, leaving us in pitch darkness.

" 'For God's sake,' says I, 'tell me where we are and what we're doing here.'

" 'Why, this here is our hideout. The train for Canada don't leave for six hours yet. And can you think of a better place to spend the time waiting than a elegant mansion?'

" 'And whose elegant mansion is it, then?' I asks.

" 'Why, it belongs to Mr. Schuyler Chauncey, the well-known society man. I was the pot-and-pan boy here for a few days once, and by some oversight, as they say, I seem to have left with a key to the house in my pocket. It's lovely, though, to have the run of the place when the family is out of town, as they is now.'

" 'But what if they come back?' says I.

" 'It ain't likely,' says he, 'since they has went to their country house in Long Branch and ain't returning for three months. No, sir, there won't be a living soul here for weeks and weeks and weeks to come, don't you know.'

"I was sure I knew. Just then, Brighteyes strikes a match and lights a bit of candle that he takes out of his coat pocket.

" 'Come along,' he says, 'and we'll see what there is to eat and drink.' Then he opens a door next to us that leads to the kitchen.

" 'Do you think you should be showing a light?' I says. 'What with this room being on the front of the house and all?' The thought that Mother Mandelbaum and her mugs may be lurking outside, you see, is as bad as being inside with Brighteyes.

" 'Not to worry,' says he. 'The blinds is all shut tight, and nobody in the world knows we is here.'

" 'Oh,' I says, 'that's encouraging, ain't it?'

" 'Right,' says Brighteyes, as he lights a lamp on the kitchen table with the candle. Then he takes off his coat and hat and begins to prowl about in the cupboards, hauling out odds and ends of food. 'Now, then,' he goes on, 'a little something to wash it down with.' And he lights the stub of candle again and walks over to a door I ain't noticed before. 'Wine cellar,' he says with a wink, pulling out another key and unlocking a huge padlock on the door. 'Come on down, and I'll show you around.'

"Brighteyes, he sticks the candle through the doorway, and I can see a flight of dusty steps leading down into what I guess is going to be my final resting place. I notice that he's got the box of diamonds with him, just in case I should consider taking a quick sample.

" 'Come along, now,' says he, all cordial and friendlylike. Then he steps through the door, and I can hear him going down the stairs.

" 'Right,' says I, 'just as soon as I wash my hands.' It was a silly thing to say, but it was all I could think of. So I run over to the sink and pump up a bit of water at the same time I'm rifling his coat. Just like I figured, his pistol ain't there—he has took it to the basement with him for obvious reasons—and there's a hundred dollars in cash and a ticket to Canada. Just one.

"Now Brighteyes is calling me from the cellar. 'Get a move on!' he yells. He ain't so cheerful now. Then I hear him starting back up the stairs. That's when I done it. I don't think about it or nothing— I just step over to the door, slam it shut, and click the padlock. It's only then that I realize the door is iron—made that way, I suppose, because of all the valuable wine that's stored down there.

"So Brighteyes has a key, but he can't use it, because the padlock is on the outside of the door, and he has a gun, but he can't shoot his way out, because the door is made of iron. He also has the diamonds, for all they is worth to him now, but

I have something better—a hundred dollars and a railroad ticket—and I wouldn't trade them for every diamond in the box at that moment.

"Well, as you might imagine, Brighteyes is now banging on the door with his pistol and shouting rude remarks. I figure that he's likely to start shooting at any moment, which probably won't do him much good as far as the door is concerned but is bound to attract considerable attention in a empty house in the middle of the night. So I depart as I had came. Mother Mandelbaum and her goons is nowhere in evidence, and I walk away with a light-hearted spring to my step for the first time since I know Brighteyes.

"I now hail a cab on Broadway, rush to the station, cash in the ticket for Canada and buy one for New Orleans, figuring that in case Brighteyes manages to find a way out of the cellar I ought to be at the other end of the continent.

"But as I'm sitting on that train headed south, I begin to have second thoughts about the thing I done. What if Brighteyes dies there alone in the cellar because I locked him in? It will be on my head, even if he is a crazy man who is trying to murder me. On the other hand, he deserves it. I am, as they say, in a agony of indecision. Finally, when I step off the train in New Orleans, I realize what I got to do, and I send a unsigned telegram to

Mr. Schuyler Chauncey at Long Branch, telling him that his house has been burgled. I figure that will do the job.

"At the time, I feel glad I done my duty, because the next day I bump into a pair of Irish fellows who invite me for a drink and I wind up in the hold of a clipper ship bound for Barbados. What with one thing and another, I don't get back to the States for three years, but that's another story altogether, and a gruesome one too.

"In any case, it ain't until I am finally back in New York that I give Brighteyes much thought. I ask around a bit, and this is what I hear: after he reads my telegram, Mr. Schuyler Chauncey beats it back to the city to see what's up. When he gets inside his house, he hears the most terrible racket—yelling and laughing and cursing and the sound of breaking glass. The society gentleman figures, quite correctly, that some maniac is flinging his rare wines against the cellar walls, and he fetches a policeman on the double.

"I understand that when Chauncey and the copper unlock the door, they find Brighteyes drunk as a lord and stretched out on a thousand dollars' worth of busted wine bottles. They say the copper is forced to shoot him in the leg to sober him up, and that it takes six months to air out the cellar. Anyways, they cart him off to jail for housebreaking, although nobody can figure out how he come to lock himself in. Brighteyes, for one, ain't talking about it. In particular, he ain't talking about the diamonds, although Mother Mandelbaum—who ain't fooled for a minute about who done it—guesses he has buried them in the wine cellar. Which of course he has done.

"I am told there is a pretty hot time around Chauncey's house for several months to come, with Mother Mandelbaum's boys standing in line most evenings to break in and find out whether she has guessed right or not. But they never get past that iron door, and Chauncey never tumbles to what is going on. Meanwhile, as a object lesson to Brighteyes, it is rumored that I'm going to be found feeding the fishes in the East River if I can be located. Being as how I am a prisoner in Barbados at the time, I cannot. Mother now dies, of more or less natural causes, and things calm down for a while. Meanwhile, Baboon Connelly and his brother Apeneck has become involved in a unfortunate incident with the police and is sent to the same prison Brighteyes is in.

"It ain't long before Apeneck enters into a heated discussion with Brighteyes about his attempt to frame Baboon, and Apeneck loses the argument. The warden is naturally upset about Apeneck's demise, although he says it is not as if Brighteyes has done in a real person. So they don't hang him or nothing—they just add another fifty or a hundred years to his sentence and throw away the key. In the meantime, I've found my way back to New York. It now looks to me as though the whole matter has pretty much took care of itself, and I go about my business in a carefree manner.

"There the diamonds sits in Mr. Schuyler Chauncey's wine cellar for twenty years, and there Brighteyes sits in the state prison, until he finally manages to break out and comes knocking on our dressing-room door. He makes me a little bargain: if I help him get the diamonds back, he won't murder us in our beds."

Pa paused and searched his pockets for his pipe. "At the time," he said, "it seemed like a reasonable offer."

·6·

"BUT DON'T you see, Pa," Vera said, holding up the box of diamonds. "This is wonderful. We've come into a fortune." She grabbed Pa and me and hugged us. "Just think what we can do with the money we get for the diamonds. New costumes. Our own music. Yes, that's it. We'll hire some musicians for the act. And maybe a composer to write songs for us." She paused for breath. "You don't suppose there's enough here to pay for a whole theater? Muldoon Hall. . . . It has a nice ring to it. . . ."

"You are demented," I said. "You should open the window and toss that box into the Hudson River. The diamonds are a jinx. Just look at what's happened so far."

"Correct!" said Pa. Then he considered what Vera was telling us. "Muldoon Hall, did you say?"

"Nothing flashy, of course," Vera continued. "Perhaps some simple country theater to get us started."

"Well, I don't know," said Pa. But I could feel him being swept away, and with him our last hope of surviving this mess intact. I went out on the rear platform of the train just as Pa and Vera were buying their first theater in Chicago. By the time we reached Cold Spring, about ten o'clock in the morning, The Merry Muldoons already owned most of Broadway.

"GRACIOUS," SAID VERA, as we stepped down from the train, "it's very rural here, isn't it?"

That more or less summed it up. Cold Spring was the hick town to end them all. The main street was lined with store buildings that seemed to have been boarded up for decades. Just across the river was the biggest mountain in captivity, which threw the whole town into perpetual shadow—more or less of a blessing, I thought.

We wandered over to the public square, a nickel's worth of untended grass by the river with a falling-down bandstand in the middle of it. Then we took a turn or two around the square. Pa had recovered much of his old bounce, tipping his hat to startled farmers' wives and pointing out features of interest with his walking stick, narrowly missing a local geezer with a forked beard and an ear trumpet. Because Pa was dressed in his green plaid suit and our valise advertised *The Merry Muldoons* in large letters, we turned heads everywhere and soon had a gallery of curious kids trailing us.

I wanted to hide. But Pa and Vera seemed to be enjoying themselves hugely, chatting with the locals like visiting royalty. For some reason there was quite a crowd in the square, and I shuddered as I realized what was coming next. After a couple of minutes, Pa mounted the bandstand and announced that we would favor them with a selection or two. He took out his banjo, and we sang "Be Home When the Clock Strikes Ten" and "What the Dickey Birds Say."

"And now," Pa announced, "fun for the little folks as Master Sam Muldoon presents his comedy clog dance."

"I'd rather not," I whispered.

"Go on," said Vera. "They'll love it."

As far as I could see, they didn't even notice it. But I'm not always the best judge of such things.

Vera ended the program with that immortal favorite, "At Midnight on My Pillow Lying." This brought a horselaugh from someone on the edge of the crowd. Vera looked annoyed and fouled up one verse, but the collection amounted to twenty-six cents in silver, a German pfennig, two or three wash-ers, and a collar button—all in all a very favorable take for The Merry Muldoons.

As Vera and I were passing the hat, Pa, spurred on by our success, made an announcement to the crowd. "And now, friends," he said, "we hope and trust that we'll be seeing each and every one of you at our grand spectacular performance tonight, to be presented at . . . " Pa was a little stumped here; he turned to a small boy next to him and asked in a stage whisper, "What did you say the name of your the-ayter was, sonny?"

"Well, sir," said the kid, "there's Steenrod's Opera House just around the corner over the grain and feed store."

"To be presented at Steenrod's Opera House just around the corner, folks, over the . . . er . . . grain and feed store—a high-class place for high-class entertainment." That brought another raucous laugh from the edge of the crowd. Pa ignored it. "Now, farewell to you until this evening. Remember, bring the family. It's refined entertainment." And he hopped down from the bandstand and began shaking hands.

"Pa, what are you dong?" I hissed at him. "We aren't performing anywhere tonight."

"True," he said. "So if we are going to eat tomorrow, we had better go and arrange it." Then he and Vera were glad-handing their way toward the theater.

"Beautiful show, Pa," I heard Vera say, as they disappeared around the corner.

"I like the way you done that song, Vera. It makes me think of the time in Jersey City when your ma and me . . . "

I was trailing along behind them, trying to remain invisible, when I heard the laugher. I turned at the sound. Standing half a dozen feet from me was one of the strangest-looking men I've ever seen—and, believe me, I've seen some strange ones.

He was well over six feet tall, with blond hair that hung loose down his back, frontier style, and a magnificent handlebar mustache. On his head was the biggest Mexican sombrero in the world, with a stuffed rattlesnake curled around the crown in place of a hatband. The man was dressed from head to toe in a fringed buckskin suit, buttoned up the front with fake-looking twenty-dollar gold pieces. Across his chest in an *X* hung a pair of leather cartridge bandoliers, and he leaned casually on a huge double-barreled shotgun, inlaid with imitation gold doodads and curlicues.

Nobody seemed to be paying much attention to the man, although he was a sight that would stop traffic on the Bowery. I gawked at him as he ambled across the street into a vacant lot and disappeared. There were a couple of horses grazing there, an Indian tepee, an old army tent, and a kind of gypsy caravan with a little stage attached to the back of it.

I followed along and read the signs on the side of the caravan. *California Dan and Dr. Floating Poplar*, one of them said in fancy big letters. And underneath it, *Kee-Nó-Toe Tonic. Nature's Gift to Nature's People.* And underneath that, *Free Show Tonight.* Now I got the point. The man was one of those quack doctors who sold his pills and potions at a free show, and he had been sizing us up as potential competition. No wonder he laughed a lot; if he was any good at all, we were going to have a quiet evening at Steenrod's Opera House. But then, we were used to that.

I walked up the street to the theater. Like everything else in town, it had seen better days. By the front door was a homemade sign advertising last night's attraction, *Murphy's Midget Minstrels, a Microcosm of Merriment and Mirth.* Murphy, as it happened, was one of Pa's pals, and we had all worked together at Sweeney's from time to time. The sign was comforting somehow, and I felt a little more cheerful. Vera was sitting on the stairs, writing in a notebook.

"Where did Pa go?" I asked.

"He found Murphy," Vera said. "They're in the saloon up the street."

"Why did I even ask?" I sat down and told Vera about California Dan. I omitted the fact that he was the one who had laughed at her songs, but I did tell her that he was likely to be our competition tonight. Vera looked uninterested.

"Come with me," she said, taking me by the hand. We climbed the stairs to Steenrod's Opera House.

"I think this theater has real potential," she said. "I believe we may buy it. I've made a few notes about possible alterations," she added, consulting her notebook. "If we move the stage to the other end . . . "

I looked around. The place was a dump, with broken windows, a potbelly stove in the middle of the room, and a flat floor filled with the sort of chairs that undertakers provide for funerals. The walls hadn't seen a coat of paint since before the Civil War. But Vera was ecstatic about the nonexistent possibilities of the place. After she finished outlining her grand plan, we tossed our bags into one of the two or three dusty dressing rooms that were jammed in behind the stage. As we did, Pa appeared in the doorway.

"Where's Murphy?" Vera asked.

"Him and his boys has gone back to New York," Pa replied. "He figures they might get our slot at

Sweeney's. Murphy said business was stone dead here for the last couple of days. There's a free show every night down by the river."

Vera looked annoyed this time. Pa sat down on a decayed trunk and leaned back against the wall. It appeared that he might begin snoring on the spot. "We got a little bit of a break, though," Pa said. "Murphy loaned me a couple of bucks, and him and me bumped into Steenrod down at the saloon. Business is so bad Steenrod is going to let us have the the-ayter for a night or two just for cleaning this place up a little. So hop to it, will you?" He yawned once or twice. "We can live in the dressing rooms . . . and we can keep all the profits. Nice the-ayter, ain't it? Wouldn't mind owning something like this." Pa tipped his derby down over his eyes and was fast asleep.

"Right," I said to Vera. "Do you want to mop or sweep?"

She and I swabbed out the place, then wandered off for a look at the local sights. There was nothing much to see, and in half an hour we headed back to the theater.

Vera and I had just started up the stairs when we were almost bowled over by a man coming down. I thought for a terrible moment that he might be Brighteyes, but he was even uglier. The man and I did one of those little clown routines: we both headed one way and then the other way and then back the first way again.

"Watch it!" he snarled.

"Watch it yourself, sir."

"Get out of my way, brat!"

On the last pass, he backhanded me into the wall and dashed past us. I was about to stick out my foot and help him downstairs when I thought better of it; he was as nasty looking a customer as I had seen since we left New York. He was wrinkled and stooped, and his eyes had a kind of mean, miserable look to them. His hair, which was no color in particular, seemed to have been hacked off close to his head instead of cut, and his arms below his rolled-up sleeves were more or less solid with tattoos. Actually, they were his nicest feature.

Once he was past us, we hurried on up to the dressing room, which looked as though it had been involved in a major railway disaster. The contents of our bags were scattered everywhere, and in the center of the room lay Pa, spead-eagled on the floor in a pool of blood.

·7·

THERE WAS a cut on the side of Pa's head, but it didn't look all that serious, and we bound it up with strips torn from an old shirt. He moaned a few times as Vera and I propped him up against the wall. It appeared to me that the man on the stairs must have come in while Pa was sleeping, bashed him on the head, and rifled our bags. I couldn't imagine what he had wanted, since our entire wardrobe wouldn't fetch ten dollars. But whoever he was, he didn't get the diamonds for a bonus, because Vera had sewn a secret pocket in her petticoat and she now carried them with her everywhere.

She and I had no theories about the crime, though we both agreed that it was certainly time to head for Poughkeepsie. Of course, Pa wasn't really up to walking, and we didn't have money to get there any other way. The only hope was that our show would bring in enough cash for train tickets.

Who did we think we were kidding? What with California Dan's free medicine show down the street, there were just five people in our audience that night, including the geezer with the ear trumpet. He must have needed it, since the whoops and hollers of delight and the constant applause from the medicine show practically drowned out our act. In the wings, between numbers, Vera raged about the unfair competition, threatening bodily harm to the medicine showman. It did not help her concentration.

To add to the fun, the tap on the head had addled Pa, who tended to have some difficulty recalling any of his lines or precisely where he was. But The Merry Muldoons soldiered on as usual. We were just heading into our big finale, in which we dance an Irish jig in our kelly green leprechaun outfits. Suddenly, Pa, who was playing the banjo, began to trail off, staring into the semidarkness beyond the footlights.

Vera shot me a questioning glance. At first, I thought it was just the bump on the head that was affecting Pa, but then I realized that he had seen something in the audience that unnerved him. He kept playing, but his timing, which wasn't much anyway, was now shattered. Vera and I were frantically attempting to dance as we peered out across the footlights, trying to figure out what Pa had seen.

"What's going on?" I whispered.

"Brighteyes," Vera whispered back. "In the last row."

Pa now wound down completely. There was a profound silence as the audience gaped in wonder at The Merry Muldoons coming apart at the seams. In desperation, Vera launched into the last verse of "When Irish Eyes Are Smiling," while Pa played something that may or may not have been "Who Threw the Overalls in Mrs. Murphy's Chowder?"

There was a ghastly little crackle of applause from the back of the house. "Bravo!" Brighteyes yelled. "Bravo, Muldoons!"

Vera now leaped to the footlights and addressed the handful of confused souls in the audience. "Thank you, folks!" she cooed. "The Merry Muldoons will be right back with another fun-filled act after a short intermission." She dashed to the side of the stage and dropped the front curtain with a crash.

I ran to her. "What are you talking about?" I said. "We've already done every song we know three times. There isn't any second act."

"Right," Vera said, heading for the dressing room with Pa in tow. "But Brighteyes doesn't know that. I imagine we have about ten minutes before he figures it out and comes back here looking for us. Let's get moving." She turned the key in the dressing-room door and shoved the old trunk up against it.

"Oh, please," I said, "let's go find Brighteyes and give back the diamonds. We'll throw ourselves on his mercy. He'll probably let us go once he has them."

"You don't believe that, do you?" said Vera, as she heaved clothes in the direction of our bags.

"I guess not," I replied. "He's going to tear us up into small bits if he ever gets close to us. But what else can we do?"

"I'll show you," said Vera. "We're leaving now, Pa." Pa was sitting on the trunk, plucking idly at his banjo and muttering to himself.

Vera pulled open a trapdoor in the dressing-room floor. "I found it this afternoon when we were cleaning," she said. "There's a ladder that leads down to the feed store. Brighteyes will think we barricaded ourselves in our dressing room, so we'll have plenty of time to get out through the store before he knows we're gone."

"And then what?" I said.

Vera looked—for Vera—a little disconcerted. "Well . . . then we'll go on to Uncle Mike's place, just like we planned. So, there you have it."

"Exactly how?"

"That," said Vera, as she started down the ladder,

"is what has to be worked out, of course. Bolt the trapdoor as you leave. I'd hurry."

She disappeared into the darkness below. Seeing no alternative, I steered Pa over to the ladder and handed him and our bags down to Vera. Then I climbed after them, pulled shut the trapdoor, and bolted it.

Somehow, our escape didn't give me a warm feeling of security. The feed store was all ominous shadows, and everywhere I looked I could see the beady eyes of the rats who called the place home. A little moonlight came in through the store windows on Main Street. We headed for it, groping our way around mountains of feed sacks, choking on the dust, until we got to the front door.

By now Pa had more or less pulled himself together. "That little blabbermouth Murphy must've told Brighteyes where we were. I'll get him for that."

"Not if Brighteyes gets us first, Pa," I said. "We have to leave here, *now*."

"Right," he replied. "I'll handle everything." He thought this over for a moment. "What do we do? We ain't got any money to take the train or hire horses."

"I guess we walk it," I said. "But I'm not sure you're in any shape for that, Pa."

"Nothing to it," said Pa. "I could walk to Poughkeepsie standing on my head."

I didn't even try to figure that one out because, just then, a big covered freight wagon rolled up Main Street past the feed store. There was a lantern hanging from the back, and by its light I could make out the lettering on the wagon's side. *J. C. Simpson, Lumber*, it read. *Poughkeepsie, New York*. The wagon jolted to a halt up the street in front of the saloon, and the driver climbed down off the box and went inside.

"Wait a minute," I said. "Maybe this is the answer. We can stow away in the wagon and ride all the way to Poughkeepsie."

"That's very good, Sam," said Vera, sounding as though she wished she'd thought of it.

"Good thinking, lad," Pa said. "I'll take charge now. Here's what we do. . . ."

"We go climb in the wagon?" I ventured.

Pa considered this. "Exactly," he said. "So let's be getting out of here."

Vera and Pa and I dashed across the street and raised the canvas flap at the back of the freight wagon. The sight was not reassuring. There was only a tiny nook left among the boards and kegs of nails and crates of hardware.

"Get in, Pa," Vera said.

"It ain't going to work," he replied. "There ain't room enough for all of us. You kids get in."

"No, Pa," I said. "We can't leave without you."

About then, the saloon doors swung open, and the wagon driver came strolling out, wiping his mustache with the back of his hand. He hadn't seen us yet, but unless we moved fast it was only a matter of time before he did.

"Get in!" Pa whispered urgently. "I'll find Steenrod and borrow enough money off him to take the train to Poughkeepsie tomorrow."

"But—" I began.

"Do what I tell you," Pa said. "Ain't I in charge here?"

"All right, Pa," Vera whispered, "but please be careful. We'll meet the train tomorrow."

"Go!"

Vera and I clambered into the wagon as Pa picked up our valise and disappeared into the alley next to the saloon. In a moment, there was a tremendous clatter as the driver worked the brake loose and the wagon lurched forward up the Main Street hill. By the time we turned north on the river road and the cargo had shifted two or three times, it was clear that Vera and I were going to be pounded to a mush well before Poughkeepsie. But at least we were on our way to Uncle Mike's.

"I don't feel good about leaving Pa behind," I gasped, as I fended off a piece of two-by-four.

"Would you rather have it be Pa in here?" Vera groaned. "This is unbearable."

We traveled for more than an hour, leaving Cold Spring behind us and heading up along the Hudson. I peeked out once or twice in the rare moments when I wasn't being attacked by a nail keg. There wasn't a house anywhere, and across the river, stretching away endlessly in the moonlight, were jagged cliffs that loomed over the water in a way that was positively sinister. To top it off, the wagon now hit a bump, driving a large bundle of shingles into the small of Vera's back.

"That's enough of that," she grunted. "I don't know about you, but I'm walking."

"I couldn't let you go alone," I said. I grabbed our carpetbag, and we slid down from the back of the wagon.

Vera and I started trudging up the road toward Poughkeepsie. After we had gone only a few yards, it began to rain. We slogged on for another mile or so, shivering and more or less asleep on our feet. Then Vera spotted a little country schoolhouse at a crossroads just ahead of us. We went inside, locked the door, and collapsed on the floor to dry out. After a while, I looked up at the window, and my hair stood on end. I saw Brighteyes peering at us through the glass. But when I blinked and looked again, there was nothing except rain streaming down the windowpane.

·8·

WHEN VERA and I got up, the morning mist off the river was just starting to clear away. We staggered outside and ducked our heads under the school yard pump. As I rubbed the water out of my eyes, I saw California Dan's caravan drawn up next to the building. I nudged Vera, and we walked over for a closer look. There, standing in the haze on the caravan's rear platform, was the giant medicine showman, draped casually around his extravagant shotgun. An Indian stood alongside him, whispering something in his ear. Not counting his warbonnet, he was at least a head taller than California Dan. The total effect was rather intimidating, as though Vera and I were suddenly shrinking.

Nobody said anything. California Dan chewed on his mustache and seemed to be studying Vera in detail. The other man could have been carved out of stone. "Soup's on," California Dan said at last, sweeping off his giant sombrero. The booming voice I had heard on the street was only slightly scaled down for the purposes of general conversation. He jumped off the platform and took Vera by the arm. Then he motioned for me to follow and headed away in the direction of a campfire on the other side of the caravan.

California Dan bowed us to seats by the fire, with rather elaborate politeness. The other man handed each of us a plate of bacon and beans, and we all began eating. It struck me that there was a kind of hardness to California Dan's courtly smile and a cynical edge to his hospitality. I had encountered it before among one or two chums of Pa's who were riverboat gamblers.

My experience suggested that Vera and I should probably eat fast, leave soon, and keep an eye on the diamonds—that is, if Vera was still foolish enough to want them after all the trouble they'd already caused. I guessed she still did. Maybe, I thought, it was like gold fever, and she was in the grip of some kind of compulsion. But I was too beaten down to think about it much.

Dan and his cohort finished eating first and sat for a while, studying us out of the corners of their eyes. The pair of them made me think of a couple of

Bowery street fighters sizing up the competition before they started heaving bricks and paving stones.

Finally, Vera broke the silence. "I'd guess by the sign on your wagon," she said, pointing to the caravan, "that you are California Dan."

"That's about the size of it," he responded. "And this is my business partner, Charlie Floating Poplar."

"Dr. Floating Poplar to you," said the other man.

"Charlie warms up a bit when he gets to know you," said California Dan. Somehow I doubted it.

"And just what is your business?" Vera asked, knowing perfectly well what it was.

"Medicine show," he answered. "Sell patent remedies, like it says there on the wagon. Give a little free show to draw in the customers. But we turn our hands to most any job that comes along. Dr. Floating Poplar and I work the territory up and down the Hudson mostly."

"Pass through Poughkeepsie, do you?"

"Heading there right now, as a matter of fact," said Dan. "Nice town, Poughkeepsie." His eyes narrowed a bit. "You know who we are now, but who are you?" he asked. He knew exactly who we were, of course.

Vera thought that one over for a bit. "We're orphans," she replied.

"Sister, dear," I said, knowing full well that nothing good was going to come out of this conversation, "we need to be moving along now. Thank the man for breakfast."

"We ran away from the orphan asylum in . . . er . . . Portland, Maine," Vera continued, emitting a rather forced hint of a sigh.

"Sad," said Dan.

She turned her face away from the showman about ten degrees and dabbed at an imaginary tear. "Hoping to join our uncle in Poughkeepsie. But it's a long way . . . a long, hard way."

"And an unusual route too," I said. Vera kicked me.

Dan was suitably shaken. "Now, now, miss. Now, now, little lady," he crooned, pacing up and down by the campfire like a melodrama actor. After a while, he struck a kind of statuary pose to suggest that he was possessed by sudden inspiration. Then he muttered to himself, shook his head violently, and resumed pacing. In a moment, he stopped to strike another pose, this one calculated to suggest resolution and finality. "I have it," he said. "I have it, little lady! You and what's his name"—meaning me—"will come along with us to Poughkeepsie."

Vera peered out at California Dan from between her fingers and quivered her chin. "Oh, sir," she said, "we wouldn't dream of imposing ourselves on you." I choked on a piece of bacon and began a fit of coughing that passed unnoticed.

"Nonsense, little lady," the showman replied. "It's the least we can do. Don't you agree, Dr. Floating Poplar?" The Indian made no visible movement. "You see," said Dan. "He is delighted that you are joining us." With that, he strode off toward his partner, who was standing motionless a few yards distant, still watching us.

The moment California Dan walked away, I grabbed Vera and dragged her behind the caravan, out of earshot. "Orphan asylum, for crying out loud!" I said. "You're as big a fraud as those two quacks. What are you trying to do?"

"I'm trying to get us to Poughkeepsie, nitwit," Vera hissed in my ear. "It's perfect. Brighteyes would never think of looking for us with Dan and Charlie's show. We just stay in the caravan until we get to Poughkeepsie and then we cut out and find Uncle Mike."

Actually, there was a certain logic to what she was saying. "But why the song and dance about us being orphans?"

Vera looked at me with disdain. "If we let them know who we really are," she said, "they might slip up and tell somebody. And it could get back to Brighteyes. Then where would we be?"

"I don't know," I replied. "*I*'d like to be back on the Bowery, and I didn't even care much for it there. We're taking a terrible chance, Vera. Dan and Charlie are fakes and cheap confidence men, and I'm positive they already know who we are. Dan watched our show in the square at Cold Spring. And, by the way, don't you think it was a bit of a coincidence that they camped here last night?"

"Fiddledeedee," said Vera. "You're imagining things again. I'm sure they don't recognize us and, anyway, I find them quite charming. Once they take us to Poughkeepsie, I even plan to forgive them for stealing our audience last night."

Just then, Charlie Floating Poplar appeared from around the corner of the caravan, smiling in an unconvincing way and motioning us inside. He had probably been listening to most of our conversation. But what, I thought, did it matter? By now, we were surely doomed anyway; if Brighteyes or the man on the stairs didn't knock us off, Dan and Charlie probably would.

Vera and I climbed obediently into the caravan and lay down on the bunks that flanked the open front door. The showmen took their places on a kind of ledge outside the door, and we started off toward Poughkeepsie. In spite of my uneasiness, it was pleasant rattling along the road with the breeze wafting in off the river. For a while, Vera kept up a steady stream of chatter. The showmen seemed not to notice. Finally, she began to snore, and I found myself drifting off.

I was barely awake when I saw Charlie Floating Poplar look back at us to make sure we were asleep. Apparently, he was satisfied, because he nudged California Dan. Then he gave him a hideous and thoroughly conspiratorial wink.

•9•

WE DROVE all morning without stopping. Vera slept most of the way, but I kept sliding into new and more creative nightmares every time I closed my eyes. After a bit, I got up and looked out the back door at what passed for scenery. There were more of those enormous cliffs across the river. On our side, there wasn't much of anything except hills and trees, a tumbledown house or two, and every once in a while a straggly little graveyard. Late in the morning, we hit a collection of decayed buildings called Castle Point that made Cold Spring look positively thriving. All in all, the scenery did nothing to cheer me up.

The inside of the caravan was more interesting but no more cheerful. There were bows and arrows and blankets and tom-toms everywhere on the walls, along with five or six million pictures of Dan and

Charlie and their cronies in various heroic poses, as well as an eerie assortment of stuffed animal heads. Before we went to sleep, Vera had slipped the box of diamonds into the mouth of a mountain lion for safekeeping.

What with Pa still in Cold Spring and my reservations about Dan and Charlie, I was feeling gloomier by the minute. But Vera had awakened at the top of her form. Not that she wasn't worried about Pa— I knew she was, even though she still refused to admit there was anything to be concerned about. But Vera had turned up the heat full blast under her girlish charm, prattling on about our totally fictitious life in the orphan asylum without even a pause for breath. After the first hour or so, Dan's and Charlie's eyes began to glaze over, and in spite of my mistrust of them, I actually began to feel sorry for the two men.

There was a map of the river valley nailed up over one of the bunks, and I started to study it so that I wouldn't have to listen to her. I concluded that we were probably going to wind up the day at another wide spot in the road called New Hamburg, and it turned out I was right. Late in the afternoon, Dan stopped the caravan next to a ramshackle barn filled with hay.

Dan explained that he and Charlie were going to do a show that night in New Hamburg. Perhaps, he said, we would like to make ourselves comfortable in the barn until it was over. He didn't wait for an answer from Vera, and I certainly didn't blame him.

From underneath the driver's seat, Dan dug out a stack of handbills advertising the show and a battered trombone, which he passed to Charlie Floating Poplar. The two were obviously ready to head into town, but Vera did not seem inclined to leave the caravan. Apparently, her fantasies had come to include herself as a star on the medicine-show circuit. "Dan," she said all too sweetly, "I believe you have forgotten something."

Dan looked at her suspiciously. "I don't think so," he said. "I've got the handbills, and Charlie's got his trombone."

"No, Dan," Vera replied. "I mean Sam and me."

"You'll be fine over there in the barn," he said. "We'll be back in a couple of hours."

"No, no," Vera continued, "I mean that Sam and I did a little singing and dancing at the orphan asylum, and we would consider it an honor to perform with you tonight."

Dan looked horrified. After all, he had caught The Merry Muldoons' act in the square at Cold Spring.

"Vera," I said, "may I speak to you privately for a moment?" I pulled her from the caravan. "What happened to your idea of staying out of sight until we got to Poughkeepsie? There's at least one man wandering around this part of the country who would like to do us in, and you want to give a public performance! I won't. Period!"

Vera stomped into the barn, muttering. As I followed her, I had the feeling that I hadn't heard the last of it, but at least we were tucked safely out of sight by the time Dan and Charlie headed into New Hamburg.

Vera sulked in a corner. Then, without warning, she began to shriek.

"What is it?" I asked, expecting to see Brighteyes leering at us from the doorway.

"The diamonds!" Vera screamed. "I left the diamonds in the caravan—in the stuffed mountain lion."

"So what?" I said. "Nobody knows that except you and me."

She paid no attention to this. "We have to go get them. Right now."

"Absolutely not," I replied. "I refuse to go. No discussion possible. We will sit here and wait, and that's that."

IT TOOK VERA only a few minutes to drag me to New Hamburg. We hid out in some weeds and tall grass across from the town square and watched Dan and Charlie as they made a couple of turns around the square in the caravan. Charlie was playing "A

Hot Time in the Old Town Tonight" as Dan scattered fliers advertising the show among a steadily increasing crowd of small boys. Soon there was a whole gallery of locals gawking at them from their front porches, with vests undone and dinner napkins still tucked into their shirtfronts.

After the third circuit, just as it was getting dark, Dan and Charlie stopped and began to set up in the square. They headed the caravan into a little clump of trees, unhitched the horses, and tied them to a tree. Then they came around the caravan and lowered the platform that was hinged to the back, creating a little stage. Dan and Charlie arranged the platform with a big Indian drum and cartons of medicine bottles that had been stored underneath the caravan. Next they lit three or four lanterns, which they hung from the roof. Gradually, the townspeople moved down off their front porches and formed a circle around them.

Soon there were fifty people or so in the square, and more were appearing all the time. One of them caught my eye. He seemed to weigh in at close to three hundred pounds. His bulk, along with the snowy white beard, ought to have made him look like jolly old Saint Nick. In fact he looked anything but jolly. The man scowled and wheezed and harrumphed as he pushed his way through the crowd and up to the medicine-show platform.

Dan, who was standing on the stage, bent down to talk to the fat man. They carried on a long conversation head-to-head, as though they didn't want anyone else to hear, and two or three times I saw Dan pointing down the river road toward Cold Spring—or, it struck me, toward the barn where Vera and I were supposed to be holed up. After a while, the man gave Dan the thumbs-up sign and pushed his way back to the edge of the crowd, only a few yards from Vera and me. There was a buggy standing in the road, and, with some difficulty, the man hauled himself up onto the driver's seat. The springs creaked and groaned in protest as he headed down the river road.

Vera was still muttering about the diamonds as Charlie began to bang on the big war drum. Suddenly, at a signal from Dan, he stopped. The silence was awesome. There was no sound but the rustle of the wind and the faint click of the beadwork fringe on Charlie's outfit. Dan bent down slowly and reached into one of the crates in front of him on the stage. When he straightened up, there was something concealed in his hand.

"Kee-ná-ka," he began solemnly, leaving a great pause between each syllable. "Kee-ná-too-ah." Whatever that meant. And then, slowly revealing the bottle in his hand, "Kee-Nó-Toe Tonic." Pause. A gesture in the direction of Charlie. "Nature's Gift to Nature's People." Then Charlie produced his trombone out of nowhere and began another ear-splitting rendition of "A Hot Time in the Old Town Tonight," which must have been the only tune he knew.

Dan raised his hand for silence once again. "Nature's Gift to Nature's People." He almost whispered the words this time, and the audience strained forward to hear him. "My colleague, Dr. Floating Poplar, pays strict attention to Nature's laws, and by so doing defies disease. Look, my friends," he continued, indicating Charlie. "Look at the health that Dr. Floating Poplar enjoys, while we suffer from—from organic derangements." He made it sound like some new and especially loathsome disease, and I could hear Vera draw in her breath at the wonder of it all. Dan was very good. "Yes, friends," he continued, "organic derangements, brought on in many cases by taking remedies directly at variance with the healthy actions of the body's system."

The spectators nodded sagely at this gibberish, as Charlie pulled out a long pipe and lit up. "While watching Dr. Floating Poplar smoking the pipe of peace," Dan went on, "let us think seriously of the habit we have accustomed ourselves to, for ages past, of freely taking deadly poisons in the hope of regaining our health." Meanwhile, everyone in front of the platform was now enveloped in a huge cloud of foul-smelling smoke.

"Turn over a new leaf," Dan implored. "Instead of treating disease by the administration of deadly poisons such as calomel, arsenic, quinine, and a legion of other hurtful drugs, commence at once and throw all such physic to the dogs. Cleanse the blood and purify the system by adopting the curative powers of Nature as Dr. Floating Poplar does—with Kee-Nó-Toe Tonic, the sponsor of tonight's big free show, presented to the good people of New Hamburg."

At this point, Charlie began banging on his drum again. Then Dan switched gears completely, performing a couple of banjo solos and a ventriloquist's routine that featured a collection of jokes so old that even The Merry Muldoons used them. The difference was that when Dan told them the audience laughed.

As they applauded, the buggy with the fat man on board rolled into the square. The driver looked grumpier than ever, and I saw him give Dan a clear thumbs-down signal, which Dan acknowledged with a bob of his head. He did not look pleased, but he never missed a beat on stage.

Now Dan switched again, launching into his first medicine sale of the evening. I must admit that the result was impressive, especially since nothing he said made any sense whatsoever. But he stomped and ranted and threatened and pleaded in the most spectacular way imaginable, sometimes fairly screaming at the audience, and at other times dropping to a whisper as he told some heartrending story of an orphan child or a careworn grandmother who might have been saved from illness, pain, and death through a timely dose of Kee-Nó-Toe. When he finished, the crowd broke into cheers and clapping, with a few "amens" and "hallelujahs" thrown in.

Dan wasted no time getting down to the sale. As the applause began to die, he dashed to the front of the platform where the cartons of Kee-Nó-Toe were stacked. He began to beat out a raucous rhythm on the war drum as Charlie grabbed a carton and advanced on the audience, selling for all he was worth. It was the first time I had ever heard him willingly say anything. "A bottle sold here, Doctor!" he yelled back to Dan. "Another bottle over here, Doctor!"

When the pandemonium was at its height around the platform, Vera gave me a poke in the ribs.

"Now's our chance!" she whispered, and we headed out of our hiding place. We executed a neat flanking movement around the crowd without anybody noticing us and came up in the little clump of trees by the front door of the caravan.

"Wait here," she said. "I'll get the diamonds."

Dan and Charlie were still at it out back, the drum beating, Charlie yelling, and the crowd cheering them on. The sale continued at a high pitch for another ten minutes or so. Then I heard Dan thanking the crowd for buying, and it occurred to me that Vera had been gone for a very long time. I crept up the steps and followed her. As I did, Vera was just heading out onto the stage through a slit in the old scrap of canvas that hung over the caravan's back door.

I rushed to the door and peered out through the canvas. Vera had grabbed Dan's banjo and marched down to the front of the platform.

"Good evening, friends," she warbled, all sweetness and light. "I'm Vera Muldoon, Dan's special guest."

"No, you're not," Dan hissed. "Get off my stage."

"My first number," Vera continued, "will be 'Listen to the Mockingbird.'" And she was off and running. Dan seemed to be transfixed. He made a little movement, as if to grab her around the neck, and then must have thought better of it. Clearly, he was waiting until the end of her song in the hope of steering her off the stage without making too much of it.

As Vera trilled away, I turned back into the dark

caravan. At the other end, filling the front door, was a shadowy figure. The figure moved toward me, and in a moment I saw a very large knife in its hand.

"I'll have the diamonds, then," said a voice with a thick brogue.

I didn't waste any time. "They're in the mountain lion," I said. That sounded idiotic. I started over again. "We hid—" The knife was coming closer. "I'll get them for you."

"Do that."

I leaped up on the bunk and put my hand in the mountain lion's mouth. There were no diamonds there. "Sir," I babbled, "that is, if you are a sir. I mean, it's so dark here that it's hard to tell what you are, and—"

"The diamonds or your life." The knife was only inches away now.

"Well," I began, "about the diamonds. . . . They don't seem to be there, actually—"

Things started to happen very fast then, rather like the cards flipping around in one of the peep show machines at Sweeney's Dime Museum. It went something like this. I am on the bunk with my hand in a mountain lion's mouth. A shadowy figure is menacing me with a knife. At that moment, there is a volley of shots outside. Audience members are screaming, and I hear three thumps from the platform, as though bodies have dropped to the stage floor. More shots striking the caravan. They frighten the shadowy figure, who lets loose an unearthly scream and lashes out with the knife, gashing me in the arm. Shadowy figure leaps out the door through which he came. I stagger and grab the canvas curtain, which tears loose from its moorings, depositing me on the stage among three bodies stretched out behind the Kee-Nó-Toe cartons and the Indian war drum. The bodies appear to be Charlie, Vera, and California Dan. Big finish. I faint. End of show.

· 10 ·

I BEGAN to come to onstage a few minutes later, in the midst of a ring of anxious faces. Vera was cradling my head in her lap, and Dan and Charlie and about ten thousand townspeople were crowded around me, offering advice and making certain that no harmful night air reached my lungs. It occurred to me that my right arm seemed not to work at all well, but Vera and the two showmen appeared to be the picture of health.

I fainted again, and when I awoke, I was lying on a bunk in the caravan, my arm wrapped in bandages and my head throbbing. Vera paced up and down the aisle between the bunks, looking tense and tight-lipped. It must have been close to midnight by then and threatening to rain yet again. The caravan, lit only by the lanterns that hung outside over the stage, was cold and gloomy, with the stuffed animals around the walls glaring at us out of the shadows. To make it all worse, Vera, who was shivering with the cold, had wrapped herself in an old army coat belonging to Charlie, which billowed and flapped as she paced back and forth, giving her an unfortunate resemblance to a bat.

Vera stopped her pacing. "It was Brighteyes who fired at us," she said. "I saw him on the edge of the crowd just before the shooting started. You must have been hit by a stray bullet."

That was not the case, of course. But it did bring up an interesting question: if Brighteyes was outside shooting at Vera and Dan and Charlie, then who knifed me in the caravan at the same moment?

Vera continued rattling away about what had happened. "I can't imagine how Brighteyes knew we were here," she said. I could imagine it. "Luckily," she continued, "he was a bad shot and missed Dan and Charlie and me. Or maybe he was just trying to frighten us. I don't know. In any case, isn't it wonderful that we have Dan and Charlie, because they are so brave and strong? Why, right now they are outside on guard, so you see we have nothing to fear." And blah, blah, blah. I was only half listening to her, but suddenly something she said struck a chord with me.

"Repeat that," I said.

"Repeat what?"

"What you just told me."

Vera looked at me oddly. "I think I said that the diamonds weren't in the mountain lion's head, because I put them back in my pocket when I went onstage."

"No. After that."

"I guess I said Dan told me that it was only a scratch on your arm, and that you would be just fine in a day or two."

"That's it."

"That's what?"

"The arm attached to the hand with the knife—it didn't belong to Brighteyes."

"You are delirious," Vera said, "and I'm going to get Dan."

"I'm all right," I said, "but I wasn't shot. I was cut with a knife. I couldn't see the face of the man who did it, because it was too dark in here, though I'll bet it was the one we bumped into on the stairs in Cold Spring. The man who attacked me had the same tattoos on his arms."

Vera looked slightly dazed. "What does that mean?"

"I don't know," I answered, "except that the man in the caravan was after the diamonds, and when I couldn't come up with them he knifed me. Maybe he's in cahoots with Brighteyes. Maybe Dan and Charlie are too, for all I know."

Vera looked unconvinced. "That's ridiculous," she said. "California Dan and Dr. Floating Poplar are perfect gentlemen who would never be associated with criminals and ruffians."

"Oh, come on," I replied. "Dan and Charlie are quacks and con men, and I guarantee you they are hiding something." I sat up for emphasis, which hurt a lot. "Look," I said, "why don't we sneak away to Uncle Mike's on our own? It isn't safe around here."

Vera pushed me back on the pillow. "We're staying with Dan and Charlie all the way to Poughkeepsie," she said. "That's final. And after we get there, who knows? Perhaps you and Pa and I will join them in the medicine-show business. It sounds like an excellent investment. Yes, I think so. I'll have to find a proper stage name, of course. I've been considering it and I believe I'll call myself Dauntless Dell La Doon."

I didn't have the strength to hit her, so I suffered in silence for a while. Vera prattled on while she prepared to lie down on the bunk across the way. As she spread Charlie's coat over her for a blanket, something shiny fell out of a pocket onto the floor. Vera picked it up and started to replace it. Then, all of a sudden, she turned dead white.

I forced myself to sit up again. "What is it?" I asked. Vera didn't answer; she came over to me, put an object in my hand, and then walked away and sat down. When I looked at it, a shiver ran through my whole body. It was a picture of Vera and me—a tintype that we had given Pa a couple of years before. He always carried it in his wallet, along with a picture of Ma.

"I knew it," I said. "Dan and Charlie are involved somehow."

Vera just sat there, shivering and staring at the wall opposite her. I struggled out of my bunk and perched next to her, still holding the tintype in my hand. "We can't be sure of that," Vera said lamely.

"No, we can't," I answered. "But Pa had the picture with him when we left him in Cold Spring, and now Charlie has it. That's enough evidence for me. Let's get out of here."

"Oh, Sam, how could we have been so stupid? You were right, of course," Vera added, choking a bit on the words, I thought. "We have to get out of here now."

"Bravo," I said.

"I'm glad you agree," she said. "I believe I have a plan."

I didn't doubt it for a minute. Vera now dropped to the floor and crawled to the rear door, the one that opened out onto the stage. She tried the knob and crawled back to the bunks again. "Locked," she said. "This may be more difficult than I imagined. But here's the idea—"

Just then I heard someone mounting the steps at the front of the caravan. Vera heard it too and froze next to me. Then she remembered the coat and rose up off the bed, slipping the tintype back in a pocket and heaving the coat onto its hook in seconds. She was halfway back to her bunk when Charlie appeared in the doorway with a tray of food. I thought he glanced at Vera a little strangely as he set the tray down. Then it seemed to me that he shot a quick glance in the direction of the coatrack.

Charlie was more than usually grim and uncommunicative as he checked out my wound. After a few minutes, I noticed him look at the coat again. Vera saw it too, and caught my eye as he all too casually wandered to the end of the caravan and leaned against the coat, meanwhile making ridiculous small talk. It was totally out of character. As Charlie went on, I saw his right hand slip behind his back and begin to explore in the region of one of the coat pockets. I was hypnotized by the sight, trying not to stare, because it suddenly struck me that Vera had slid the tintype back in the wrong pocket. A glance at her, and I knew she realized it too.

In a moment, a rather quizzical look passed over

Charlie's face as he discovered that the picture was not in the right place. He made some vague excuse about the night getting colder and took the coat down from the rack, put it on, and shoved his hand into the other pocket. There was a momentary look of relief. Then he frowned and shook his head slightly, as though dimly aware that the picture had been in the wrong place. Turning on his heel, Charlie wished us a rather unconvincing good-night, went out, and pulled the front door shut after him.

As he exited, Vera was already on her feet. She drew back a corner of the curtain that hung over a glass panel in the door and peered out for a moment. Then she tried the knob and came scuttling back to my bunk. "Dan and Charlie are sitting on the front steps," she said, "but Charlie didn't lock the door. That's good. Now, just do what I tell you, and everything will be fine."

I certainly couldn't figure out what her plan was. The walls and floor of the caravan were made of oak planks, and there were no windows in the side walls, only a solid glass panel in each of the doors and a kind of skylight like those in the roof of a Pullman car—a lot of small windows set into a recess running the length of the ceiling. The skylight windows opened out for ventilation, but there was no way for me to get through one with my wounded arm, even if the windows were big enough.

I noticed Vera studying the skylight with some intensity. "It's useless," I said. "I couldn't possibly make it."

"I know that," Vera answered, "but I could."

"Wonderful," I said, "and leave me here to be strung up by my toes by Dan and Charlie."

"Oh, be quiet and help me," Vera whispered. She carried a high stool that stood in front of Dan's desk into the middle of the caravan. I steadied the stool as well as I could while Vera climbed up on top of it. In a moment, I felt her tap me with her foot to signal that she wanted to get down.

"I can do it," she said. "If you grab me around the legs and shove a bit, I can make it through the window."

"Then what?"

"I'll tell you about that as we get ready." Vera moved around the caravan gathering up our things and tossing them into the carpetbag as she explained in a stage whisper what she had in mind.

"No," I said. "You can't possibly do it. I won't let you."

"Of course you will. We don't have any other choice."

I was struck by her logic. We didn't have any other

choice that I could see, so I shut up and waited. We spied on Dan and Charlie through the glass panel in the front door for half an hour or so, during which time neither of them budged from the steps. At last, Dan finished a cigar and pulled out his watch. Then, after a whispered word with Charlie, he set off across the square on some errand or other. This was the break we needed.

Vera and I moved fast. In ten seconds, she was on top of the stool with her head and shoulders out the window. At one point, there was an ominous rip, but Vera wriggled forward and soon was halfway out. She began to kick and thrash, and I knew she was stuck. With my one good arm, I shoved as hard as I could on her legs, and in a moment she popped through the window onto the roof outside.

I could hear her crawling along the top of the caravan. When she reached the back near the stage, there was no sound for a time. Then I heard her signal, a faint tapping on the roof, and I jumped into a bunk and pulled the covers up over my head, as Vera had told me to do. In a second, all hell broke loose as she tossed one of the lighted lanterns that hung over the stage into the box filled with bottles of Ke-Nó-Toe. As Vera had guessed, the Kee-Nó-Toe was mostly alcohol, because the broken bottles shortly began to erupt in geysers of blue flame. Some actually exploded in a highly satisfying manner.

Next, I heard Charlie leap off the front stairs and come running around toward the stage. As the din grew louder, there came the faint sound over my head of Vera scuttling back along the length of the caravan. I got the front door open just in time to see her clambering down one of the fancy brackets that supported the roof. I watched first one leg and then another come into view, followed by her arms as she hung for a moment from the roof's edge. She dropped quietly to the ground and signaled to me that all was well.

In two minutes flat, we were running down a pitch-dark side street leading out of town. Behind us, shutters and doors were slamming open as the sound of the explosions woke the people around the square. Somehow, it brought back the moment, not so long ago, when Brighteyes burned down the Schuyler Chauncey mansion and set all of this unpleasantness in motion. But it seemed better not to dwell on that. After three or four blocks, Vera and I stopped to catch our breath. Looking back, we could see flames licking the sky above the square. Vera daintily dusted off her hands. "So much for California Dan and Dr. Floating Poplar," she said.

· 11 ·

I WASN'T at all sure that Vera had it right, but it didn't seem like the time to debate the issue. "Let's get going," I said.

"Nothing to worry about," Vera answered. She leaned on a gate in front of a shabby little house and began to shake a stone out of her shoe. "The way I figure it," she continued, "it will take them an hour or so to put out the fire. Chances are they won't even think of us until it's out, and by then we'll be—"

"The way I figure it, Dauntless," I said, "they're looking for us right now." I pointed down the road toward the square, where a group of men with torches and lanterns, led by Charlie Floating Poplar, was already starting in our direction.

"Oh, my," said Vera. She quickly opened the gate, and we squatted down inside the fence. We poked our heads up and looked around for someplace to hide. It didn't seem too hopeful. Vera and I were on the edge of town, and all we could see in any direction were garden plots and open fields. There was no reason to believe that the crowd had seen us; maybe they had just made a lucky guess about which way we went. But now they were searching front yards a block or so away, and in minutes they were bound to stumble over us unless we found a hiding place.

There was only one thing to do, and both of us headed automatically for the shabby house. I slid open the front door, which, like the doors of all small-town houses, was unlocked, and we eased our way into a bare hall. A little moonlight came through the transom, and we could see a door, partly open, leading into a shadowy parlor on our right, and another one, firmly closed, at the end of the hall, with a ribbon of light streaming out from underneath it. Behind it, we could hear wheezing and coughing and snatches of conversation.

I crept up to the door at the end of the hall and squinted through the keyhole. It was the kitchen, and seated at a table I saw a man in a nightshirt filling most of my view. With unerring instinct, Vera and I had chosen to hide out in the house of the sinister fat man from the town square. He was talking to another man who was outside my range of vision.

Just then, there was a tremendous pounding on the front door, accompanied by a babble of voices that suggested half of New Hamburg had gathered in the front yard. Vera and I dived through the parlor door. The moonlight coming through the front window revealed a tacky little room with nothing much in it except the usual horsehair-covered settee and chairs, a center table, and a tall glass-fronted cabinet next to the fireplace. As we looked around, there was more wheezing and coughing and more scraps of conversation, this time coming from the hall. Then the front door opened, and somebody, apparently the two men from the kitchen, descended the steps to the front yard.

Vera and I crept to the window and, peering out through the fringe on the shade, saw the fat man—and California Dan. Facing them were Charlie and the townspeople. Charlie looked hot and tired and cross, his face stained with soot and his fancy outfit singed and blackened by the fire. From time to time, he pointed down the street in the direction of what was left of the medicine show. I could only hear the occasional word, but it was not too difficult to determine that Vera and I figured prominently in his speech to Dan. All the while, Dan was pacing back and forth, growling to himself, and the fat man was wheezing grumpily and tugging at his suspenders in an attempt to pull a pair of trousers up over his nightshirt.

After a few minutes, the fat man shambled back into the house, heaving himself up the steps as though he was mountain climbing. Dan followed. The crowd was still milling around in the yard, making a lot of noise, but Vera and I could hear Dan and the fat man talking in the hall, just outside the parlor door. "You take the diamonds," Dan said, "and welcome to them. They've been nothing but trouble from the beginning. But I want those brats myself, and when I get them—"

The rest of his statement was blessedly drowned out by the crowd. It was clear enough anyway, I thought. At least, it proved that I'd been right all along about Dan, though I couldn't make out why he wanted to hand over the diamonds to the fat man. Maybe the fat man was going to deliver them to Brighteyes, or to the man with the tattoos, or to somebody else in their gang. Maybe the men in the yard with Charlie were gang members too. Maybe there was a whole town filled with people who were after the diamonds—and us. And here we were, trapped in the middle of them. I could imagine a lot of possibilities, each one uglier than the last. What I couldn't imagine, of course, was what actually happened next.

Dan and the fat man exchanged a few more pleas-antries outside the parlor door and then headed off toward the kitchen. Eventually, the kitchen door slammed behind them, and I breathed a little easier. But in a moment, the door opened again. I could see a light and hear Dan and his cohort heading back down the hall.

"I gotta get my gun," I heard the fat man mutter, and I was struck by the curious sinking sensation that comes when you are about to realize something awful that you've conveniently blotted out. Then it struck me with full force: it was a gun cabinet that stood next to the fireplace, and at any moment the two men would be walking through the parlor door.

Vera and I both looked frantically around the little room for someplace to hide.

"Is there a closet or something?" Vera whispered.

"No," I whispered back.

"How about the fireplace?"

"Boarded up. Maybe we can go out the window."

I crept over to it, knowing in advance what I would find—the cracks had been painted over for decades, and there was no way to open it except with a crowbar.

"Center table," Vera said, diving for it.

It seemed to be the only hiding place. The table had a ragged shawl draped over it that didn't reach the floor at some points, and there wasn't really room for two of us and our carpetbag. But there was a chance we wouldn't be discovered as long as the room stayed fairly dark. In any case, it was our only possibility except surrender or a fight we were bound to lose.

Vera and I crawled under the table, twining ourselves around a forest of carved curlicues on the base, with me holding our bag between my knees, which were jammed into the general vicinity of my earlobes. I drew the side toward the cabinet. Vera was smart; she took the opposite side and could stretch out a little without too much danger of being seen.

For a while, nothing much happened. I could still hear conversation from the hall over the sound of the crowd outside the house, but nobody came into the parlor. After about five minutes, I was in agony, with every muscle at war with every other, and an ugly case of pins and needles in my feet and legs. But I didn't dare shift my position.

In ten minutes or so, just as I was deciding that I couldn't bear it another second, the door swung open to admit the two men. I could see them clearly through a hole in the shawl. The fat man was holding a candlestick and a large ring of keys in one hand. In the other, so help me, was a whole pie, which he was casually munching on as someone else might nibble on a sugar cookie. He set the candle and pie down on the table above our heads and, from the sound of it, began to sort through the ring of keys, meanwhile grunting and growling at Dan through a mouthful of pie.

Apparently, the fat man was in no particular hurry, and with every moment my agony increased. The table seemed to be sprouting lumps and bulges in new and unexpected places, and the tingling in my legs and feet was advancing rapidly northward. I knew that I *had* to move; it was not a question of wanting or not wanting to do it; my muscles were offering no other choice. Without warning, my right leg shot out from beneath the shawl, and I dragged it back. Then my left arm began to twitch and knock up against the base of the table.

The fat man, who had opened the cabinet and gone back to his pie, heard the noise and jumped— if that is the appropriate way to phrase it in his case.

"Whazzat, Dan?" he asked through a mouthful of pie.

"What's what?" Dan replied as he removed a double-barreled shotgun from the cabinet.

The twitching resumed. Now my shoulders were bobbing, and my head began to bang against the underside of the tabletop.

The fat man heard the sound. There was a small note of alarm in his voice this time.

"Hear 'at, Dan?"

"No." Dan loaded the shotgun with a pair of shells and snapped the breech shut.

At this point, I began to lose all control, and my head knocked up against the tabletop with a resounding clunk that probably sent the candle jumping into the air.

"Ye gods, Dan," yelled the fat man. "It's spirits."

It was at that moment that I made my decision. I shoved hard on the table, sending it careening into the fat man, and at the same time grabbed Vera by the hand. I'm not quite certain what happened then, because the candle went out as it hit the floor. But as I reconstruct the event now, it seems likely that the fat man skidded on the remains of the pie and fell backward onto Dan. This apparently caused the shotgun to go off. The blast knocked down a portion of the ceiling, which collapsed on us, filling the room with plaster dust and turning all of us chalk white. I could see Dan and the fat man struggling to untangle themselves.

Vera now leaped up, grabbed our bag, and dragged me to my feet. I was moaning in agony from the pins and needles. The fat man, hearing my moans and seeing two white figures rising up next to him, recoiled in horror and fell back again, imprisoning Dan under his enormous bulk. Vera pulled me into the hall. I was just about to open the front door and start hobbling down the steps when Vera almost jerked my good arm out of the socket. She managed to turn the key in the lock just as someone on the outside began to pound frantically on the door. Then she dragged me down the hall in the opposite direction—to the kitchen.

She peered through the screen door. There was nobody outside the kitchen, and Vera and I headed away from the house, running through vegetable gardens and pastures, north from the edge of town. Maybe running is not the right word in my case; I stumped along while both of us flailed at our hair and clothes, trying to get rid of the worst of the plaster dust.

After a while, we struck the main road along the river. Looking back toward New Hamburg, we could see the men from the front yard of the fat man's house heading up the road in our direction. Dan and the fat man were leading the pack. They were easy to spot because they glowed slightly in the moonlight. But it occurred to me that Vera and I did too, so we holed up a few hundred feet away near the ruins of an old house. Nothing much remained of it except for a chimney and a big cellar hole filled with rainwater, but we found a place to hide in the yard, in an overgrown grape arbor, until the men passed by.

Vera and I waited for fifteen or twenty minutes

after they disappeared up the road. "Well," I said, "what now?"

"You could give me the diamonds."

"You already have them," I replied. "They're in your pocket."

"I didn't say anything," Vera answered.

"I did," said Brighteyes, rising up behind us in the grape arbor. As usual, he was pointing a gun at Vera and me. He looked more cuckoo than ever. "Now, then," he said, prodding me with the gun, "I'll be grateful if little Vera will hand me them diamonds, real careful-like."

Vera looked pained, but she did it.

"Very nice," said Brighteyes. "Now, if you two delightful children will walk over to that cellar hole, I will shoot you both and dump your bodies in it. It will give me great pleasure to do that." He savored the thought for a moment and then frowned. "But, as always, you has made extra work for me. I'll have to weight your bodies down with stones first so as they don't float. It wouldn't do for anybody to find you until I'm away with them diamonds, now, would it?"

"Absolutely not," I said. "It would spoil everything."

"Right," Brighteyes replied, "and we wouldn't want that. So if you'll just move over by the cellar quicklike. The two of you will have plenty of time to think over the error of your ways once you is at the bottom of that there hole." He prodded me again, and as he did my heart leaped up for an instant; from behind us, I heard the sound of a gun being cocked.

Then a voice came out of the darkness. "Not two, Brighteyes," said the disembodied voice, "but three." And out of the vines stepped the man with the tattoos. He had a rifle trained on us.

Brighteyes looked confused. "And just who the devil might you be?" he asked.

"Don't you know your old pal, Brighteyes?" asked the man.

Brighteyes peered at him for a moment through his thick glasses. "Could it be?" he said. "Could it be Michael Aloysius Connelly himself? Could it be Baboon Connelly? Sure now, it couldn't be, because Baboon Connelly is still rotting in prison for his misdeeds."

"Wrong, Brighteyes," said the man. "He busted out just after you did. It is Michael Aloysius Connelly himself, in the flesh, come to do you in and take the diamonds that rightly belongs to him."

"My dear boy," said Brighteyes, "we'll want to talk this over."

"No, we won't," said Connelly. "You tried to frame me and you murdered my brother. You and them brats is going to wind up at the bottom of the cellar hole, and I am taking them diamonds."

"Ah, but Baboon, lad," said Brighteyes, "we *will* want to talk because, you see, while you are pointing a gun at me, I am also pointing one at you. And not only am I a better shot, I am crazy as a bedbug and will try anything. You may plug me, but you will surely die in the attempt."

Baboon puzzled over this for a moment. "You may have a point there," he said.

"Dear Baboon," Brighteyes replied, "I do have a point indeed. Co-op-er-a-tion, that's the ticket here, ain't it? You and me and them diamonds will be on our way to Canada in no time at all. Let me explain it to you. . . ."

By now the two of them were nose to nose near the edge of the hole, and very much absorbed in their discussion. But it was clear that Brighteyes was still making some attempt to cover Vera and me at the same time that he kept his pistol aimed at Baboon.

"Ushpay?" whispered Vera in pig latin.

"Onay!" I gasped.

Brighteyes turned in our direction.

"Esyay," she retorted. "Ownay!"

There was nothing to do but join her. We hit Brighteyes and Baboon about knee level, sending them catapulting backward into the cellar hole.

There was a considerable splash as they hit the water. Brighteyes was still clutching the box of diamonds as he fell. It sailed out of his hand, and Vera made what, in all fairness, can only be described as a sensational catch over the edge of the hole. The result was that she came close to joining Baboon and Brighteyes, but I pulled her back from the brink just as a bullet from Brighteyes's pistol whizzed past my right ear. There were a few gasps and gurgles from the cellar, and then a beautiful silence as the two goons sank slowly into the mire.

A s BABOON and Brighteyes disappeared from sight, the skies opened with the cloudburst that had been threatening all night, and Vera began to cough and sneeze uncontrollably.

"I can't stand it," she said at last. "This is too much. It has been raining every ten minutes since we left Sweeney's. I have to go someplace where I can dry out."

"We don't know what's up the road," I said. "There may not be a house for miles."

"Then we'll go back to New Hamburg."

"Fine with me," I said. "I'm for anything that will get us out of here before Brighteyes and Baboon surface. But aren't we likely to run into Dan and Charlie and the fat man?"

"Not if we stick to the fields," Vera replied, between sneezes. "They're still looking for us on the river road. And who else is going to be out in weather like this? Come on." She tossed the box of diamonds into our bag, grabbed me by the hand, and headed back toward town.

I was too tired to care one way or the other, so I slogged along with her. We stayed a couple of hundred yards away from the river road, halfway up a hillside, traveling through cornfields and pastures. The ground was steep and rocky, and I seemed to fall over a fence into the mud every few feet. After a dozen bouts with various kinds of barbed wire, I was about to give up and lie down in a ditch. But Vera drove me on until we stumbled back into the outskirts of New Hamburg.

A block or so in front of us was the public square where Brighteyes and Baboon had tried to murder us. The caravan was still smoldering a little in the rain. But Vera was right; not a soul was out. There were lights in a couple of the houses around the square, though the half-dozen stores and other buildings were all pitch-dark. The nearest one was a scruffy little brick structure, by the river, set away from everything else. We ran for it and peered in the window. It was an office of some kind, and there didn't appear to be anybody there. We opened the door and went inside. Something struck me as a little odd about the place, but it wasn't until I went exploring that I realized where we were.

Vera was rooting around in the dusty little office

as I opened a door at the back of the room. Ahead of me was a corridor with a bare brick wall on one side and two tiny cells on the other, with their doors standing wide open. We'd picked the local jail to hide out in. But I imagined that it didn't matter much, since there were no other customers and there were not likely to be any in the middle of a thunderstorm.

The corridor was shadowy and grim, with only a tiny square of gray light coming through a single barred window across from the cells. I peered into one. The door was a heavy grating of iron straps with a kind of hinged bar that ran across the front and fitted into a hasp on the wall. Hanging loose from the hasp was the biggest padlock I'd ever seen. The door would have held in a maddened elephant with no difficulty.

There was nothing in the cell except two tiny bunks hung from one of the dirty walls, with an old blanket folded up on each. But considering some of the places Vera and I had been spending our time recently, the place looked downright luxurious. It was damp in the cellblock, and the temperature seemed about twenty degrees lower than outside. I grabbed one of the blankets and sat down on the bottom bunk to rest for a moment. I vaguely remember Vera wandering in and climbing into the top bunk. In a second, I could hear her snoring. And then I was dead to the world, dreaming about that gigantic iron door, which seemed to close with a sinister slam as I rolled over and sank deeper into sleep.

I DON'T KNOW how much later it was when I finally began to wake up. A couple of hours, I guess. When I came around at last, Vera was still sawing wood in the bunk over my head—and the cell door was firmly shut. Of course, the carpetbag was missing too. I leaped up, staggered over to the door, and stuck my head out between the bars. Sure enough, the giant padlock was in place and locked tight. I could see a light and hear somebody moving around in the office up front, but I couldn't push my head forward far enough to get a glimpse through the office door. We were prisoners once again, and I didn't even know who had caught us this time.

It took a while, but I finally managed to get Vera more or less awake. I told her what had happened. "I'm too tired to deal with it," she said as she flopped back on the bunk. Then, almost as her head hit the pillow, she sprang back up, wide awake. "What did you say?" she asked, dropping down from her bunk.

I told her again as she headed for the cell door and began to shake it. "Hello," she yelled. "Who are you? Why did you lock us in?"

There was no sound from the office for a moment. Then I heard a chair creak violently, and someone started walking across the floor in the direction of the cell block. Next, I saw a huge shadow on the wall across the corridor, and wheezing and puffing, the fat man appeared in front of our cell door, with a shotgun cradled in his arms.

"You two," he said sourly, "are too dumb to be believed."

"What!" screeched Vera.

"You heard me, dummy," the fat man continued. "Just when everything was fixed up real good, you had to go and mess it up."

"You monster," growled Vera, pointing at the gun. "You fiend. Go on—finish us off. Get it over with."

"Oh, clam up," said the man. "And listen to me, or you'll wish I had finished you off."

Vera now launched into one of her Queen of Tragedy routines. "Don't think we don't know what's going on," she moaned. "You and Dan and Charlie are all in this together."

"Correct," said the fat man, as he opened our cell door. "That we are. And we would've worked things out real good if you two hadn't fouled it all up. Ain't you ashamed of what you done to Dan and Charlie and I? Their caravan is a wreck, you blew up two hundred dollars' worth of Kee-Nó-Toe, and you made a fool of me in front of everybody in New Hamburg—in an election year, no less. Now get into the office. March."

Vera ignored him. "We demand our property back at once."

"You mean them diamonds? Fat chance."

"They belong to us."

"The devil, you say. The whole world knows you two little rats pinched them off of Brighteyes Dunphy. That was a big mistake—he's crazier than a coot. You'd be dead by now if it wasn't for Charlie and Dan."

I was beginning to get the feeling that Vera and I had reached one or two wrong conclusions somewhere along the way. "Mister," I said, "could I ask you one question?"

"No."

"Please?"

"All right. One."

"Who are you?"

"Say, you don't know much, do you?"

"No, not much."

"I'm the sheriff of New Hamburg, laddie," he said, turning on his heel and starting to waddle away. "Now get in the office."

"Mister," I said, following him down the corridor, "can I ask one more question?" I didn't wait for an answer. "Aren't Dan and Charlie quacks and confidence men?"

"Of course," said the sheriff, "but they're decent fellows, for all that, and they done everything they could to keep you and your pa from getting killed.

Remember that when you're accusing them of being crooks." He paused and looked rather piercingly at us. "There's some," he said, "who might wonder whether you two ain't the crooks."

"The diamonds are ours by right of treasure trove," Vera said haughtily. "If you want them, you will have to contact our attorneys."

"Bull," said the sheriff. "Them diamonds is going back to the police in New York, and you two is going to your uncle Mike's until I catch Brighteyes. It's a miracle you ain't fish bait by this point. But you will be if you don't go into that office fast. I guarantee it."

"Wait a minute," said Vera. "How do you know all these things about us?"

"I guess you're about to find out," the sheriff replied. "Now move it."

It was still dark, and the office was lit only by a single candle on the sheriff's desk. But it wasn't hard to pick out Dan and Charlie, slumped in the shadows, looking soggy and distinctly unfriendly.

"I curse the day I ever set eyes on the pair of you," said Dan, "and I want you out of my life."

"Set down and shut up," said Charlie, "or we will probably feed you to the hogs." His position seemed clear enough. Vera and I sat down and shut up.

· 13 ·

"I JUST GOT one question," said the sheriff. "Who the devil is that other crazy man with Brighteyes? We seen them on the river road an hour or so ago, but they got away from us. The two of them looked like they had just crawled out of a swamp."

"Not exactly," I said, "but close." I filled them in about Baboon, and what Vera and I had done at the cellar hole.

There was a long, painful silence. Finally, I broke it because I was beginning to feel terrible about everything that had happened. "Sheriff, Charlie, Dan," I said, "I'm sorry about all the trouble. I really mean it. Vera and I didn't understand—"

"I agree," said Vera. "But that is in the past. I want all of you to know that I believe you now. I don't think you're part of Brighteyes's gang. You were just trying to help—in your way."

"That's very bighearted of you," said Charlie.

"I would also like to make clear," she continued, "that Sam and I were wrong to do all of the things we did. We beg your forgiveness." She turned to me with a steely glint in her eye. "Tell everyone how sorry you are, Sam."

"I thought I had."

Vera paid not the slightest bit of attention. "Right," she said, turning back to Dan and Charlie. "And that goes double for me. Now, then—you know where our pa is. The sheriff said so. Tell us."

"Don't tell her anything," said Dan to Charlie.

"We apologized," said Vera. "You have to tell us about Pa."

"No," said Dan. He turned to the sheriff. "Take them back to their cell, Earl." Dan leaned over Vera and spoke to her with a certain grim finality. "You are going to your uncle Mike's in the morning. That is all you need to know."

"We won't go," said Vera.

"Could we talk about that—" I began.

"Hush!" said Vera. She turned to Charlie. "We're not going unless you tell us about Pa."

"Forget it," said Charlie. "Your pa said to take you to your uncle Mike's, and that's where you're going. You ain't safe here with those two lunatics on the loose. Especially after what you just done to them."

Vera turned back to Dan. "Tell us about Pa," she demanded. "Or we don't go."

"You're going to Poughkeepsie," yelled Dan.

"Pa!" cried Vera.

"Poughkeepsie!" Dan bellowed back.

This went on for some time. Dan caved in first. "All right," he said. "We'll tell you if you'll just put a sock in it for two minutes." He gave Vera a withering look. "After our show ended in Cold Spring, Charlie and me walked uptown for a drink at the saloon. Just as we passed the alley next door, we heard a groan. That's when we found your pa. He was cut up something terrible—but I recognized him from that awful show you put on in the square earlier."

Vera looked outraged, although she didn't say anything.

"Is Pa all right?" we both asked at the same time.

"Well, at first Charlie and me figured he was more or less done for," Dan continued, "but we picked him up anyway and took him around the corner to Doc Poston's house."

"He looked real bad," said Charlie, "as pale as death from all the blood he lost. But the doc said he'd probably be okay if he stayed in bed for a month or two. I'm standing over your pa when he opens his eyes and looks up at me.

" 'Brighteyes,' he mumbles.

" 'Right,' I says. 'Hope you get along fine. We got to go now.'

" 'Brighteyes,' he says again. 'He didn't get the diamonds.'

" 'Correct,' I says, having no idea what he is talking about. 'You just have a good rest, and the diamonds will be fine.'

"Well, at that point Dan and me turn to go out of the room, but your pa puts up such a holler that we come back again. 'The kids,' he says. 'You got to save them kids.' "

"After a while," Dan continued, "Charlie and me get the story out of your pa—about how you two left town in the freight wagon, and how Brighteyes jumped him in the alley and cut him up when he found out he didn't have the diamonds. Your pa said he figured you were well on your way to your uncle Mike's in Poughkeepsie by then. The way I figured it, Brighteyes had probably seen you get into the wagon and had done you in already. But your pa seemed like a nice fellow, so I didn't say nothing except that Charlie and me would have a look for you.

"That's when your pa give Charlie the tintype," Dan continued, "the one you found in his coat pocket later on. 'Don't tell them kids what happened to me,' he says. 'Just make sure they get to Mike's place. Brighteyes will murder them unless you do. Promise me you'll get them kids to Poughkeepsie. I'll meet them there as soon as I can.'

" 'I promise,' I says. 'We were headed up that way anyhow. Now go to sleep.'

"As we were leaving, he says, 'You two fellows watch out for them kids.'

" 'We'll find them for you,' I says. 'I promised you.'

"Then your pa begins to laugh hysterical-like. 'That ain't what I mean,' he says. 'You don't know them kids. They ain't like other people. But you'll see. You'll find out.' " Dan looked at Vera and me darkly. "I didn't understand what he was saying then, but I sure do now."

"The long and short of it," Charlie added, "was that we started up the river road looking for you. When we got to the schoolhouse, a man was peering through a window at you, but he disappeared into the fields as soon as he seen us. It must've been Brighteyes, of course, and he must've been all set to break in to the schoolhouse and walk off with the diamonds. And Baboon must've been somewhere out there too, just waiting for his chance to get Brighteyes and have the diamonds all to himself. But we didn't know about Baboon then. Anyhow, we pulled the caravan up next to the schoolhouse and took turns guarding you until you woke up."

Charlie paused for a moment. "Once you did, we

begun to have second thoughts about taking you to Poughkeepsie. If you don't mind my saying so, right away you begun to look like . . . er . . . too much for us to handle."

"I don't believe I understand you, Charlie," Vera said coyly. "Sam and I enjoyed your company immensely, didn't we, Sam?"

"Ummp," I replied. I recognized with a sense of horror that she was starting in with her girlish charm routine.

So did Dan and Charlie. But they carried on bravely under the circumstances. "That's why we left you in the barn outside New Hamburg and got hold of Uncle Earl," Dan said. "We figured it was time to get the law involved."

"He's your uncle?" I asked.

"I don't know how I could have done such a thing to my own flesh and blood," Dan replied. "But I did it and I'm sorry. Earl, he agreed to take over and get you to Poughkeepsie. Of course, you weren't in the barn when he got there—you were at the caravan preparing to get stabbed and shot at and that sort of thing."

"But why would Brighteyes shoot at me?" Vera asked. "He still wouldn't have the diamonds even if I was out of the way."

"I don't think he was aiming at you," Charlie said. "I believe he was trying to knock off Dan and

I. That way, he would have you and the diamonds all to himself again. And that's why we were standing guard outside the caravan after the show—you remember, just before you burned it down—"

"Oh, fiddledeedee," said Vera. "That's all forgotten now, isn't it? We have to think about the future. Once Pa's on his feet again, I thought perhaps we might all"—with a twitter—"team up together." She turned to Dan. "I believe that you and I could work up an act. We could call it California Dan and Dauntless Dell, Snappy Songs and Witty Patter. What do you think of that?"

Even Charlie seemed amused at this one, and Dan was making a considerable effort not to double over with laughter. "No offense intended," he said at last, "but I would rather drink a bottle of Kee-Nó-Toe than ever appear onstage with any of the Muldoons again. And I would do almost anything to avoid drinking a bottle of Kee-Nó-Toe. That stuff is terrible."

Vera looked decidedly grim and seemed reluctant to continue the conversation. It was very quiet in the office for a while.

"Well, now," she said at last, "we ought to be starting soon."

"We ought to be starting *what* soon?" the sheriff asked warily.

"The trip to Cold Spring," Vera replied, heading for the door. "To fetch Pa."

Just then the door flew open, and a boy about my age, soaking wet and miserable looking, came into the office.

"What do you want, Elmo?" the sheriff growled.

"I brung a note from Doc Poston in Cold Spring," he said, placing a soggy piece of paper in the sheriff's hand.

"Give him a nickel, Dan," said the sheriff as he read the note. "Now, get out of here, Elmo." Elmo retired reluctantly into the rain with his nickel.

"Don't bother about Cold Spring," said the sheriff, dropping the note into Vera's hand.

"It's no bother," Vera replied.

"It's no use either," said the sheriff. "I hate to tell you this, but your pa has disappeared."

·14·

"PA HAS *what*?" Vera said.

"Read the note," said the sheriff. "Doc had a deputy guarding your pa's room. But the deputy fell asleep last night, and when he woke up your pa was gone. That's all anybody knows."

"Brighteyes," Vera yelled. "Brighteyes got him. Or maybe Baboon."

"Maybe," the sheriff said. "Or maybe not. Who knows at this point?"

"We have to find our pa," Vera said.

"No," said Dan, "*we* have to find your pa. Charlie and I are going back out to look for him now. *You* have to go back in that cell and set there until Earl takes you to Poughkeepsie in a couple of hours."

I waited for the explosion. But it never came. Vera paused, thought it over for a moment, and then process. The box was not in any of them. There were a couple of broken-down cupboards in the room, and she rifled these next, strewing papers in every direction, practically burning her fingers but finding nothing. The noise she was making would have awakened the dead.

"For heaven's sake, be quiet," I whispered. "The sheriff will hear you."

"What difference does it make?" Vera replied, pulling the key to the padlock out of her pocket with a flourish. "He's locked up tight."

"But not *too* tight," I said. "He has the other key, remember? He can get out of that cell anytime he wants to."

"Oh," said Vera. "I hadn't thought of that."

"I guessed you hadn't," I replied.

At that point, two things happened more or less simultaneously: Vera spotted the box with the diamonds, which was in plain sight on the mantelpiece, and there was a bellow of rage from the cellblock as the sheriff, who had awakened and discovered what was going on, came careening through the door into the office, shotgun in hand.

Vera made a dash for the diamonds, but I grabbed her and dragged her out the front door into the usual downpour. We were about a quarter of a mile along the river road when Dan and Charlie's caravan, somewhat charred, appeared out of nowhere. Char-

nodded. "Correct," she said. "That's the way to do it, isn't it?" Vera stretched and yawned extravagantly. "Well, time to hit the old hay," she cooed at me. "Come along, little fellow, and I'll tuck you in. Say good-night to the gentlemen, Sam."

"Er . . . good-night," I said.

"And thank you all for your stimulating company tonight." Vera curtsied—she actually curtsied—as she swept me off down the corridor toward our cell. My heart shriveled with fear.

"Stay alert," Vera whispered. "The time is near."

"What's that gibberish supposed to mean?" I asked.

"Nothing," Vera replied. "I didn't say a thing."

The sheriff, who was a few steps behind us, seemed unconvinced. "You wouldn't be hatching some new plan, would you? Like blowing up the caravan again or setting fire to Charlie Floating Poplar?"

"Nonsense," Vera replied, over the thunder that was rattling the jail once again. "We will retire to our cell now," she said grandly, pulling the door closed behind us. The sheriff locked the door and headed for the office, muttering to himself. I could hear him talking to Charlie and Dan for a while, then the outside door opened and closed, and the medicine men were gone. The sheriff came huffing and puffing down the corridor again with his shotgun tucked under his arm, peered at us for a moment through the bars, and then disappeared.

"We will leave in an hour," Vera whispered. "He should be sound asleep by then."

For a moment, I was frozen with horror. "Excuse me," I babbled at last, "but I don't want to leave here. This is the first time I've felt safe in a week."

"And what about Pa?" Vera said. "Is he safe out there in the storm, cold and alone?"

"Now stop that, Vera," I whispered.

"Don't trouble yourself," she continued. "Just lounge in your bunk in comfort while I"—here she did her best imitation of a tubercular cough—"while I go out looking for our pa. He will understand. Good-bye, Sam. Good-bye. I'm coming, Pa."

"All right," I said, "you're breaking my heart. But how can either of us go anywhere? We're locked up, and the sheriff is standing guard over us with a gun."

"I am always amazed at your lack of foresight," Vera replied, recovering nicely. "Before I went to sleep, I found the spare keys to this place in the sheriff's desk. So I hooked them. After all, one has to be prepared for everything. I don't suppose he'll notice they're missing, do you?" And without waiting for an answer, she swung herself up into the top bunk and closed her eyes. "Wake me in an hour," she said.

Vera was right on the mark. In an hour, the she iff's snores, from somewhere nearby, were shakin the whole building. Vera, meanwhile, was holdi her own in the snoring line from our upper bur What with the wind howling, the rain thudding the roof, and the thunder crashing outside, the eff was terrifying. I pulled the blanket over my he but it didn't help, so I gave up and shook Ve couple of times to bring her around. She blin once or twice and then climbed down from her b and unlocked the padlock on our cell door.

By a flash of lightning outside the cellblock dow, I could see that the sheriff was slouche the lower bunk in the other cell, with his he his chest, fast asleep. Vera closed the door sheriff's cell, which made an unearthly screec snapped the padlock shut. The sheriff mum few times, but he didn't wake up.

We tiptoed past him and entered the o headed for the outside door, but Vera poun our carpetbag, which was lying open on the the sheriff's desk. She struck a match. "I kr she said, rooting away in the bag. "The di aren't here."

"Fine," I replied. "I wish the diamonds appeared long ago. Let's leave."

"Not so fast." Vera began pulling out drawers, one by one, making a terrible rack

lie was slumped on the driver's seat with his coat collar turned up around his ears and water cascading off the brim of his hat. Dan was standing in the doorway behind him, looking disagreeable. Vera and I dived for the bushes and took off running into the woods nearby. The caravan rolled past us without either of them looking in our direction, but it was a close call.

"We have to get off the road," I said.

"Don't bother me," Vera said. She looked distracted.

"There's the barn where Dan and Charlie left us before," I said. "I suppose that will do for the moment."

Vera didn't even hear me. She was trudging along like a sleepwalker. I took her by the hand, and we slogged our way through the rain and went inside.

"The diamonds," Vera muttered. "It's more than I can bear. I tried so hard, but somehow . . ."

"Never mind that," I said. "Let's figure out what to do."

Vera looked at me blankly. She was a million miles away. "I'm too depressed to think," she said. "I'll work out a plan as soon as I have a rest. I suddenly feel very tired. I don't understand what has happened, and I . . ." She tucked the carpetbag under her head and closed her eyes.

"You can't go to sleep, Vera," I said.

"Rmmmp," Vera replied, as she burrowed deeper into the straw on the floor.

At this point, there was nothing to do but go to sleep myself, and I was afraid to, so I went exploring. The place was certainly gloomy in the middle of a storm, with only slivers of light coming in between the boards that covered the outside of the barn. But it was dry and in better shape than it looked. It seemed to be used by some farmer for storing hay. There were bales of it piled almost to the ceiling in some places and great mounds of loose hay spilling out of a loft overhead. In a corner, I found a ladder that led to the loft. I climbed up, stripped down to what was left of my underwear, spread my wet clothes out to dry, and draped an aged horse blanket over my shoulders. Then, of course, I fell asleep too.

WHEN I WOKE UP, hours later, the weather had cleared a little, and a weak sun was just starting to set. Vera was still asleep on the barn floor. As I climbed down the ladder to wake her up, she let out an unearthly yell and leaped up.

"What's the matter?" I shouted. "Is it Brighteyes? Where is he?"

"No," said Vera. "It isn't Brighteyes."

"Well, what *is* it?"

"It's me. I see it now."

"I don't," I replied.

"I had a terrible dream," Vera said. "I was running down some muddy road in the dark, and it was raining and cold, and somebody was chasing me."

"Brighteyes?" I asked.

"No," said Vera. "That was the worst part. It wasn't Brighteyes."

"Well, who was it?"

"I just told you," Vera replied. "It was me." She sat down in the straw, and I could see a tear start to trickle off the end of her nose. "I understand now. It was me. I caused all of this."

I sat down next to her in the straw and tucked the horse blanket around her shoulders. "It's all right," I said.

"No, it isn't all right. I only wanted to help the family, but I just couldn't stop. I went too far. I always go too far. I didn't have any right to do the things I did, and now look what's happened. We're going to be murdered, and maybe Pa already has been, and I've made everybody's life miserable, and . . . and . . . it rains all the time! It never stops raining!" She burst into tears.

I put my arm around Vera's shoulder. "It wasn't just you," I said. "It was me too. I'm as much to blame as you are. And . . . and . . . we're never going to see Pa again." I confess there may have been a tear or two dripping off my nose too. I got up and walked over to the barn doors so Vera wouldn't notice. But I think she did, because she came over to me and put the horse blanket around both of us. We stood in the doorway for a while, looking out at the lane that connects the barn with the main road, not saying anything.

I guess I saw him first. There, trudging up the lane, framed by the rays of the setting sun and looking very much the worse for wear, was our pa.

•15•

ERA AND I rushed out of the barn and threw our arms around Pa. "Oh, my dear children," he said, "I was sure I would never see your faces again." Then he fainted dead away.

We carried him inside, as gently as we could, laid him down on a couple of bales of hay, and closed the barn doors. Vera bathed his face with water from a pump nearby. After a while, he came around, groaning and sputtering.

"Pa," Vera asked, "why aren't you still at the doctor's house?"

"I sneaked out," he said wanly. "Had to find you. Oh, I feel terrible, just awful." He turned his head in my direction with some difficulty. "Maybe I got up a bit too soon. Do you suppose that could be it?"

"Could be," I said. "But how did you find us?"

"Well, now, there ain't nothing very complicated

about that. After I sneaked out of the doc's place, I just begun walking toward Poughkeepsie. Got as far as a little place up the road called New Hamburg this morning. Now here I am—and mighty glad to see the pair of you too."

"But Pa, how did you know we were here?" Vera asked.

"I didn't, you see," he answered, which seemed to clinch the matter for him. Vera looked confused.

"Wait a minute," I said to her. "Let me try it another way." I turned to Pa. "Now," I said, "please tell me how you knew where to look for us. It's important."

"Sure and I didn't," Pa answered with a look of mild annoyance at our obtuseness. "That is to say, I didn't but I did, after a manner of speaking."

"Oh. . . ."

"Pa," Vera said, slowly and with great deliberation, "please tell Sam and me who told you where to find us."

"It was that nice fellow Charlie. I bumped into him in New Hamburg. He was with that pal of his, Dan."

"Pa," I said, "Charlie didn't know where we were, did he?"

"Well, not exactly. Charlie says to me, 'If you don't find them on the river road, look in the old barn outside of town.' Then Dan, he says, 'I bet they *would* pick a damn fool hiding place like that, and I hope they done that because they're not where they're supposed to be and I want to see them real bad.' I don't know what he had in mind, but they'll be along to get us soon."

I thought Vera looked distinctly anxious. "I wonder," she said to nobody in particular, "whether we shouldn't be moving on now."

Pa continued to ramble. "I had a bit of trouble finding the barn, but I met another fellow on the road who was real helpful. Didn't get his name, but he looked familiar somehow. He was real interested in everything I had to say about Charlie and Dan and about you two kids."

"Any tattoos?" I asked casually.

"Yeah," said Pa, brightening. "Pretty ones. You know him, then?"

"Not well," I said, "but he *is* interested in us."

"Oh, Pa, no!" Vera wailed. She turned toward the barn wall, but I was way ahead of her, already peering out into the twilight through a crack. There was no mistaking them: Baboon and Brighteyes were there waiting for us. They were making a half-hearted attempt to conceal themselves in the tall grass twenty or thirty yards from the barn, but every once in a while an old familiar mug would pop up over the grass and leer in our direction.

"It's both of them," I whispered to Vera.

"What's that?" asked Pa cheerfully.

"Hush!" Vera and I said in unison.

Pa looked annoyed and began to mutter to himself.

"We could sneak out the back," said Vera.

"What back? The only doors are in the side of the barn facing them."

"Windows?"

"There's only one, and it's in the hayloft. If we tried to jump out, we'd break our necks. But the loft is an idea. The sun's almost down, and it will be dark enough up there that they may miss us. If we're lucky, Dan and Charlie might get here in time."

Vera blanched a little, but she agreed. "Come along, Pa," she said.

"I'll do no such thing," he said, "until I know who's out there."

"All right," Vera replied. "It's Brighteyes and another old pal of yours, Baboon Connelly."

Pa puzzled over this for a moment. "I thought them tattoos looked familiar," he said. "Which way is the hayloft?"

I grabbed the bag, and the three of us established a new record in indoor ladder climbing. From the loft window, we watched Brighteyes and Baboon creeping up to the barn, occasionally tripping over each other and falling flat. After a while, it got too dark to see them any longer, which was a relief of a sort. Finally, we heard them slide open the barn doors and come inside.

It was not difficult to follow their progress. First, there was a deafening crash as someone collided with a piece of farm machinery, and then a kind of hollow boom as an empty milk can upset and went rattling across the floor.

"Watch it," said a voice.

"Watch it yourself."

"Hayrake on the left."

"Whose left, you idiot? Ouch!"

"*Watch it!*"

And so on, as Brighteyes and Baboon inched their way around the inside of the barn until they were directly under the trapdoor to the loft.

"Ladder," someone whispered.

"Where?"

"*There*, you nitwit!" It was Brighteyes talking, and we could hear him start up the ladder.

"Dig!" whispered Pa, who was burrowing like a mole into the gigantic stack of hay that filled the loft.

"I don't think I would—" I started to say, just before the whole haystack shifted and began to pour down over the three of us.

There was a muffled shriek from Brighteyes as the torrent of hay reached the trapdoor, sucking him down the ladder like a drowning man caught in a whirlpool. That was the last sound I recall hearing before the hay closed over us. In a second, I was coughing and choking from the dust and enveloped in darkness. I began to dig frantically, pushing with my legs and wiggling along like a worm in its tunnel. Once I tried to call out to Vera, but it only brought on a fit of coughing.

At last, just as I was about to give out, I bumped up against something hard and unyielding. Out of sheer terror, I gave whatever it was a terrific shove and felt it move a little. I shoved again; this time the thing seemed to tip away from me. Then there was a tremendous crash—I had been pushing against half a dozen bales of hay stacked up, one on top of another, on the edge of the loft. All of them went plummeting onto the barn floor below.

The rush of hay that followed deposited me, unhurt but gasping, on the floor of the barn. I scrambled out from underneath an avalanche of hay just in time to see Vera and Pa careering after me, riding on their stomachs as though they were sledding down a snowy hill.

When they hit the floor, I dragged them, snarling and sputtering, to where they could breathe. Bright-eyes and Baboon were nowhere to be seen, and it dawned on me that perhaps they were buried somewhere under the hay. Then I began to hear muffled grunts and see the surface of the hay moving a little at one point. It seemed likely that Brighteyes and Baboon would eventually dig each other out and survive, but at least we had a head start. I grabbed Vera, who grabbed Pa, and the three of us hobbled off down the lane beneath—wonder of wonders—a clearing sky.

·16·

PA AND VERA and I passed through a pasture beyond the barn into a patch of woods on the New Hamburg side. As we stopped for a second to catch our breath, I could see that the woods spread out into a ravine between us and the town. We half ran, half slid down it for three or four hundred yards. When we reached the bottom, we found a creek winding its way between one hill and another dead ahead of us. We were just figuring out whether it was safe to cross when I heard a horrendous crashing behind us. Brighteyes and Baboon. There was nothing to do but plunge in and head for the other side, splashing across in hip-deep water.

"What now, Dauntless, old girl?" I asked, hoping that the question would penetrate beyond the fog of gnats and mosquitoes that was engulfing our heads. I was worried about Vera; she seemed . . . smaller somehow.

"Up the next hill," she said dully. "I think New Hamburg is on the other side."

I glanced at Pa, who was draped over a stump, gasping for breath. "Can you make it, Pa? The town is just over the hill."

"So am I, lad. So am I," Pa answered, as he staggered to his feet and began to climb.

The hill loomed larger and darker as time wore on, but we struggled forward, boosting Pa over the roughest spots, until we were halfway to the top. We stopped there to listen for Brighteyes and Baboon, who by this time seemed to be thrashing around in the creek below.

At last, exhausted and dripping and swatting at the swarms of insects that surrounded us, we reached the top of the hill and looked around. Of course, there was no town there. We were lost.

The woods stopped abruptly at a fence a few feet in front of us, giving way to what was surely the largest cow pasture in the Western Hemisphere.

"Town's right on the other side, I'm sure," Vera panted.

"How do you know?" I gasped.

"Well, it has to be, doesn't it?" She sounded unconvinced.

I shrugged. Pa just breathed heavily. There was a long pause.

"We have to do *something*," I said at last. Our choices appeared to be to strike out across the pasture, where we could easily be seen in the moonlight, or to slog through the fringe of woods that ringed it. "I don't know about you," I said, "but I vote for crossing the pasture. Still, we're sitting ducks if Brighteyes and Baboon get to the top of the hill before we reach the other side. What should we do, Vera?"

She just stared at me. "I don't know," she muttered. "I just don't know. . . ."

It struck me that somehow I was now in charge. "It's okay," I said.

Vera nodded gratefully.

"Let's go through the pasture," I said, with a courage I didn't feel. "We'll make a run for the tree with the big rocks around it in the middle of the field."

"But, I think—" Pa began.

"Come on, Pa, Vera. We can make it. Keep low, everybody."

The rocks turned out to be a herd of cattle bedded down for the night. I tried to stop running, but it didn't work. I collided with a very large and irritable cow. In my view, cows have an undeserved reputation for gentleness and a live-and-let-live attitude.

Vera and Pa and I were suddenly in the eye of a hurricane of flanks and moos. Cattle seemed to be moving in every possible direction at the same time, as if to grind us to a pulp on the pasture floor.

A few yards away was the big old tree I'd spotted from the woods. I dragged Pa and Vera toward it, bouncing off cows all the while. There was a fork in the tree only a few feet off the ground, and I boosted them into it and crawled up after them. The cattle were scattering in all directions around the field, and I began to think that we might be able to move on again in a few minutes. But just then, Brighteyes and Baboon emerged from the woods into the pasture at about the same point where we had entered. There was no chance of us running for it now without them seeing us; all we could do was to climb higher in the tree and wait it out until they had a look around and went on their way.

We inched up another ten or twelve feet, where the leaves made us almost invisible, and settled down to wait. As we climbed, I could see Brighteyes and Baboon split up and disappear, searching the fringe of woods along the two sides of the pasture. I saw them again as they reappeared at the far end.

I thought they'd move on then. But back they came in our direction, walking perhaps fifty yards apart, searching the grass in case we were concealed there. The cows sensibly ignored them. Brighteyes and Baboon passed our tree without ever looking up and continued on until they had covered the entire length of the field. Then they repeated the whole process, about twenty yards apart this time.

"All right," Brighteyes called to Baboon, after their third sweep, "I give up. Come over and set for a bit."

With that, the pair of them converged on our tree and flopped down at the base. Why it was that those two lunatics would spend an hour combing every inch of the countryside and then neglect such an obvious hiding place was beyond me. But they just stretched out on the ground, grumbled at each other for a while, and drifted off to sleep. They were soon snoring loudly.

Vera was nodding off too. I leaned across from my branch and nudged her. She shifted her position slightly, sending down a shower of twigs and bark. The snores stopped for a moment and then went on.

I elbowed Vera again. "We can't stay here. If they sleep until daylight, they'll see us."

"If you'll let me sleep until daylight," she mumbled, "I don't think I care. I deserve Brighteyes and Baboon."

"Nonsense," I said. "We're all going now, Vera. We really are."

"Go quietly."

I turned desperately toward Pa. He was out cold. I tried shaking him but only managed to send another two or three tons of debris pouring onto Baboon and Brighteyes. The snoring stopped again.

"Whazzat?" one of them muttered.

"Cows. Izz cows."

"Uhhh."

The snoring commenced a third time.

"For heaven's sake," Vera whispered, "you're sure to wake them if you do that." Her speech was heartening. There was a touch of the old Vera there yet.

"Then help me, Vera," I implored. "I have no talent for this kind of stuff. Save us. You're the only one who can do it."

"Whatever you like," she said, brightening visibly. "But tread lightly, will you?" She managed to get Pa awake, and the three of us started down the tree, with Vera in the lead.

Now, I don't know whether you have ever faced the challenge of maneuvering three people and a carpetbag down an oak tree in the dark without making any noise. But assuming you have not, I am here to tell you that it can't be done—even by Vera Muldoon, a quarter of an inch at a time, which is the way she did it that night. Yet in spite of the squeaks and moans and squawls that resulted, not to mention the hail of vegetation, Baboon and Brighteyes remained peacefully asleep.

Then, as we tiptoed away, Vera stepped on Brighteyes's hand.

• 17 •

WHILE BRIGHTEYES nursed his hurt fingers, Baboon roped Pa and Vera and me to the trunk of the big oak. Vera didn't even struggle.

"I'm sorry, Sam," she sniffed. "I've done it again. My failure is complete, isn't it?"

"It's all right," I said. "Everything's going to be fine."

"No, it ain't," said Baboon cheerfully, as he tightened a knot. "At least, for the three of you it ain't. Now stow the gab or you'll wish you had."

We stowed it. Nobody was feeling very talkative anyway. Around daybreak, Brighteyes and Baboon wandered a few yards away, out of earshot, and held a conference. Judging from the grunts and snarls that floated in our direction, they were not in complete agreement about something or other. But after a bit, they seemed to resolve things, and Baboon came back and untied me and led me over to Brighteyes.

"Congratulations, lad," Brighteyes said. "You have been selected to tell me where the diamonds is. This special honor comes your way because you appear to be the only one in your family with any shred of common sense, and I believe you will recognize at once what will happen if you don't talk."

"If you kill us all, you'll never find the diamonds," I said, testing the water a little.

"True," said Brighteyes, "but you will also be dead."

"How do I know you won't get rid of us anyway?"

"You don't," he replied, with a ghastly leer, "but take it from me, lad, my word is my bond." He paused. "Or don't take it from me. But it's the only chance you've got. I reckon you understand that."

"I reckon I do." My stomach was beginning to rotate in an ominous fashion. It was clear that he was planning to do in the lot of us, wiping out the chief witnesses against him, except for Baboon. And I wouldn't have given much for Baboon's chances either.

I thought it over for a moment. Of course, we had left the diamonds on the sheriff's mantelpiece, but

I wasn't going to set Brighteyes on his trail—we had done enough to him as it was. Still, I thought we might be able to buy a bit of time if my plan worked out.

"All right," I said. "Vera and I had the diamonds in the barn, but they got lost when the haystack collapsed. Hard to tell just where they are, though."

"I figured you might say that," he responded, eyeing me craftily.

"Of course, you'd want to check it out before . . . er . . . you let us go."

"Oh, right," he said. "I'd want to make sure you was being straight with me about it and all. Still, it might take some time to find them—like looking for diamonds in a haystack, as you might say."

"You can depend on me, Brighteyes," I burbled. "They're right there in the barn somewhere."

"Correct," he replied. "Now cut the talk so I can tie you up." He grabbed me, dragged me back to the others, and roped me up with them again.

"I'll just go and have a look for them diamonds in a bit," he said, "and I'll be leaving Baboon in charge of you until I come back." He bent down for a confidential word with us. "You may have noticed Baboon ain't too bright, so I'm going to take a extra precaution or two to make sure you is still here when I get back." Then, with a parting snigger, he turned and headed off across the field to a tumbledown little shed on the edge of the woods that I hadn't noticed the night before.

He went inside and came back carrying what appeared to be an armload of kindling wood. That didn't make much sense to me unless he was planning to burn us at the stake, which seemed unlikely but not inconceivable, considering this was Brighteyes. But as he came closer, I could see that toasting a few Muldoons over a bonfire was not what he intended.

I don't suppose it's possible for a person's blood to freeze in his veins, but mine performed a good imitation as I realized that what he was carrying was a load of dynamite. It was probably used by the farmer who owned the field to blow up rocks, but it was clear that Brighteyes had something else in mind.

In a moment, he was back among us, whistling some quaint old tune as he fastened the dynamite sticks to us and ran a wire over to a detonator just inside the woods, thirty or forty yards away. If Pa and Vera and I showed any signs of unusual activity, all Baboon had to do was push down the plunger.

I had to admit that the plan was altogether worthy of Brighteyes. I didn't imagine that he'd allow Baboon to blow us up until he actually had his hands on the diamonds, but I couldn't be sure. He was crazy, after all. Anyway, the dynamite would certainly discourage any attempts at escape we might cook up in Brighteyes's absence. But in fact, we were already discouraged enough: Pa was inert, and Vera, though she tried to hide it, wept softly as the grisly work progressed.

At last, Brighteyes disappeared into the woods with a cheerful wave in our direction, leaving Baboon hovering menacingly over the detonator. Baboon stumped up and down for an hour or so, looking mean and self-important, alternately glaring at us and shooing the cows away. Then he settled down under a tree with a terrible cigar that I could smell even in the middle of the pasture. After a few minutes, I saw Baboon's head start to bob, and he began to nod off.

I could certainly understand the impulse, since none of us had had any decent rest for the better part of a week. But I found myself wide-awake and unusually alert. As Baboon dozed under the tree, you see, he began to tilt sharply in the direction of the detonator, which was only inches away from him. Every once in a while, he would give a little twitch and jerk upright and then fall over toward the detonator again. With every new spasm, he came a little closer to the plunger.

Nobody said anything, but I could sense that Pa and Vera were also watching this ghastly pantomime. Soon Baboon was sound asleep, and with each passing second he was slumping further and we were moving closer to our Eternal Home. It was sort of fascinating to watch, but nerve-racking.

Finally, Vera broke the silence. "I can't stand it," she hissed. "He'll hit it any second now. I'm going to scream."

"Which will guarantee he hits it," I whispered. "Please don't do it."

"I can't help myself. I'm going to scream."

"Vera, don't."

She let out an absolutely earsplitting shriek, which of course caused Baboon to topple over in the direction of the detonator—and as he did, a hand reached out from the tree behind him and plucked it away, while another hand snaked forward and grabbed him around the throat.

The hands belonged to Earl, who shortly came slogging across the field in our direction, bouncing Baboon in front of him by the shirt collar and holding a pistol to the man's right ear.

"How did you find us?" Vera asked.

"How could I miss?" said Earl sourly. "You don't have to be no great shakes to follow a trail like the five of you left. Them woods will take years to grow back. Now, let's get you out of here before Brighteyes pops up again."

It was a trifle late for that, though, because at that

moment Brighteyes stepped out of the woods with a gun in each hand, firing a few shots over our heads for effect.

Then he walked calmly over to us and smiled pleasantly. "Drop the pistol, Fat Man," he said to Earl. Earl dropped it. "I been right out there in them woods the whole time," Brighteyes said, turning to me. "You didn't imagine I'd fall for that haystack business, did you, now?"

"Well, actually, I did," I said, "but—"

"Enough of that," Brighteyes interrupted, turning to Earl. "Now let Baboon go," he said. "And what's that I see in your coat pocket, Fat Man? You got them diamonds, ain't you? I figured you might. Hand them over, or else."

There didn't seem to be much room for argument. Earl hesitated for a second, then unhanded Baboon, reached into his pocket, and pulled out the box.

"Open it up," said Brighteyes.

Earl did, and there were the diamonds, twinkling away in the early morning sunlight.

"A beautiful sight," Brighteyes said to Earl. "Now put the box on the ground next to your pistol and back up against that tree with the rest of them screwballs. I'd tie you up too, but there ain't enough rope in the world to do the job." He repeated this witticism three or four times, and then looked around for Baboon, who was nowhere in sight now.

"Oh, Baboon," he called, "would you kindly just step over by the tree for a moment?" He turned back to us and cocked both pistols. "I hope that everybody will understand if I take this opportunity to solve all my problems at once." Brighteyes tapped his foot impatiently. "Baboon!" he bellowed. "Get over here now!"

Baboon's response floated back from the edge of the woods, where he had taken shelter behind a tree. He stuck out one hand to reveal the detonator as he spoke. "Just sling them diamonds over here, Brighteyes," he called, "or I'll blow the lot of you to smithereens."

Brighteyes was shocked. "Now, Baboon, old chap," he began, "let's think this through."

"I already done that," Baboon yelled back. "Toss me them diamonds, or else."

"I won't!" screamed Brighteyes.

"You will too!"

"Won't!"

"Then say your prayers, Brighteyes!"

I could see Baboon's other hand now, rising up over the plunger. He was going to do it, diamonds or not. I gritted my teeth and waited for the blast to follow. But just as Baboon's hand swept down in an arc, there came a resounding bellow from behind him that stopped him in his tracks.

"Touch that thing and *you* die, Baboon."

Baboon considered the offer and then set the detonator down on the ground as Charlie and Dan appeared next to him, shotguns leveled. Simultaneously, Earl picked up his pistol from the ground and knocked Brighteyes over the head with it. It made a satisfying *thunk*.

AFTER A FEW minutes we got everything sorted out. Charlie and Dan and Earl untied us and trussed up Brighteyes and Baboon with the leftover rope. We hauled them to the edge of the pasture and sat down to rest a while in the shade. We were an unhealthy-looking group. Vera, in particular, seemed done in by the whole affair.

"I want you to know," she said to Earl, "that I . . . I'm sorry for everything I did. I mean it. Take the diamonds and give them back to their rightful owner."

"There probably ain't one," the sheriff replied. "You can file a claim when you get back to New York, and I imagine you'll wind up with them eventually, after the state takes its cut. Not that you deserve it."

Vera smiled wanly. "Thank you, Earl." She reached up and gave him a kiss on the cheek. "You're a nice man," she said. "And you're nice men too," she added, advancing on Dan and Charlie.

They did not seem to hear her and walked rapidly away into the woods.

"What's that about them diamonds?" asked Pa, who was sitting nearby.

"We left them under the oak tree," said Vera.

"Don't trouble yourself. I'll get them for you," Pa replied amiably. Then he got up, stretched a bit, took a step or two forward, and tripped over the detonator, which nobody had remembered to disconnect. The resulting blast more or less annihilated the oak. As for the diamonds, they were last seen heading west in the direction of New Jersey. That was when Vera fainted.

I SUPPOSE, in a way, everything did turn out more or less all right, after all. In a little while, Brighteyes and Baboon were shipped back to Sing Sing Prison, and Pa and Vera and I were back at Sweeney's Dime Museum, doing our usual twelve shows a day. Pa recovered from his wounds, and Vera eventually became her same old irrepressible self once again. As I said at the beginning, she decided to make the best of the whole business by turning our adventure into a dime novel, which was to be called, I believe, *Dauntless Dell's Daring; or, The Curse on the Casket of Diamonds.*

Vera threw herself into her writing. After a few days, however, she became feverish and fitful and began to mumble to herself and stare at her notes for hours. Every once in a while, though, she would be seized by some sort of creative frenzy, which generally resulted in her crossing out most of what she had done the day before and writing twice as much.

At last, she seemed to crack under the strain and took to her bed. Finally, she shoved the manuscript—now grown to tremendous size—into the stove in our flat at Sweeney's. Not, you understand, that Vera totally abandoned her newly found literary ambitions; as you know, she simply transferred them to me. I guess I didn't really mind, since it was for Vera.

After a while, I finished writing this book. Vera thought that we should send copies of the manuscript to everyone concerned, for comments. I will spare you the criticisms, except to say that generally the responses have been most unenthusiastic. Perhaps one or two are worth mentioning, though. Earl says the book will never sell, because nobody will believe there are such idiots in the world. Pa says it will never sell, because there are too many big words in it. Dan and Charlie have not answered Vera's letters, so we are not certain how they feel.

I know how I feel. I would like to have a little rest; the Brighteyes Affair has taken a lot out of me—especially the last part where I wrote this book while doing twelve shows a day at the dime museum. Maybe the book will be my ticket out of show business, after all. That would make everything worthwhile, I suppose. But just barely.

Oh, yes, one other thing. For some absurd reason, Vera felt that Brighteyes and Baboon ought to read the manuscript too. But both copies came back from Sing Sing marked *Addressee Unknown*. That worries me a little.